KILLER INSTINCT

Matthew Wade knew the border freightline business well. But when his enemies set him up with a wagonload of guns that didn't work, he knew that surviving wasn't going to be simple. But it was a darn sight easier than leading Don Diego into the formidable Sierra Madre, facing a trumped-up murder charge, and fending off a young *señorita*. And if that wasn't bad enough there was the old friend who kept wondering if Wade still had that killer instinct that once might have made him the fastest gun alive.

CLAYTON NASH

KILLER INSTINCT

Complete and Unabridged

LINFORD
Leicester

First published in Great Britain in 2001 by
Robert Hale Limited
London

First Linford Edition
published 2002
by arrangement with
Robert Hale Limited
London

British Library CIP Data

Nash, Clayton
  Killer instinct.—Large print ed.—
Linford western library
  1. Western stories
  2. Large type books
  I. Title
  823.9'14 [F]

  ISBN 0–7089–9947–6

Published by
F. A. Thorpe (Publishing)
Anstey, Leicestershire

Set by Words & Graphics Ltd.
Anstey, Leicestershire
Printed and bound in Great Britain by
T. J. International Ltd., Padstow, Cornwall

This book is printed on acid-free paper

1

'Nits Breed Lice!'

He knew he should have killed Kendrick when he had the chance, but instead he threw a hitch on his killer instinct and beat the hell out of the son of a bitch.

It was a mistake. Nearly a fatal one.

But Matthew Wade didn't realize that until later — much later — when it was almost too late to do anything about it.

The trouble was, he couldn't really touch Kendrick, even though Wade himself was freightline boss for Marc Brennan's Rio Bravo Freight Company, operating between San Antonio, Texas, and Monterrey, Chihuahua, Mexico. He couldn't fire Kendrick because he was Brennan's troubleshooter, couldn't dock his pay, and sure as hell couldn't lecture him in the hope that the man

1

would never again pull the same lousy trick.

So that left a bullet or fists.

Wade chose fists and it's a fight they still talk about in Laredo . . .

It started because of the goods in Number Three wagon on the southern leg of the run from Corpus Christi to Laredo. They had been warned to watch out for bands of rampaging Indian renegades, made up of Apache, Caddo and Comanche with a few maverick Cherokee and whites thrown in for good measure.

Attacks on the freight wagons were nothing new: Wade had been fighting off Indians or outlaw whites for months, for the rich Mexicans in the Monterrey — Guadalupe area spared no expense bringing in extravagant goods for their wives and families — and, in some cases, mistresses.

On this particular run he didn't expect any attack, though, for it was mostly perishable goods — flour in casks, smoked bacon, coffee, bags of beans and the like — but he didn't know there had been a big army raid on the Indian hide-outs that had driven the survivors into rugged, inhospitable country where food was not easily obtainable.

Steve Kendrick knew, though. And as part of his job was to safeguard the freight, he took his own steps and didn't see fit to advise Matthew Wade of them.

They were south of Beeville and crossing the murky Nueces River near its entry into Lake Corpus Christi when the renegades hit. It was much further south than their previous raids and maybe the freighters weren't quite as alert as they should have been, but the renegades struck when all three wagons were in the water.

It was good strategy on the renegades' part, but it was no place to be fighting loaded wagons across the slippery river bottom, muddy water frothing into your lap as you struggled to use your mount to keep the big

Conestogas on the safe underwater trail.

The first wagon was close to the far bank and it was the relief driver, standing to look back over the weathered canvas canopy, who spied the attackers sweeping in from both sides. He yelled a warning and next instant clawed at his red-seeping throat before spilling into the shallows. The echo of that first shot was drowned in a thunderous volley, and bullets tore holes in the canvas, splintered wagon-sides, and a couple found their targets. A mule in the second team reared and honked shrilly, tangling in the traces, dragging its companion half under water. This mule, too, began thrashing and shrilling, eyes wild, ears jerking in panic. Froth surged around them as the big wagon's momentum took it almost on top of the downed mule. The driver fought desperately, his sidekick busy shooting at the yelling renegades. There were a couple of trash whites amongst the raiders; Wade drew bead on one with his hot Winchester and blew the man out of the saddle. His next shot took an Indian in the arm and the man's gun fell as he reeled, reined his mount aside.

Wade's hat spun off his head, revealing his thick fair hair hanging down his neck. He crouched in the saddle, using his knees to control his wild-eyed horse to some extent, heeled it in on the far side of the wagon and used the cover to hurriedly thumb home half a dozen bullets through the loading-gate. The canvas shredded and one of the iron hoops rang dully as lead ricocheted from it. He heard more shots thudding into the heavy casks of tallow and flour and other goods stacked inside, hoping none of the coal-oil containers would be holed; spilling oil could destroy their edible cargo faster than bullets . . .

He urged his mount around the tailgate, saw the relief driver stretched out on top of sacks of beans, emptying his rifle into the wheeling, screaming

5

ranks of the attackers. They hit the river in a huge fan of spray — and that was their mistake.

They plunged in upstream from the wagons, no doubt figuring to allow the current to carry them down on the hapless freighters. But the water was deep there, deep enough to force the horses to swim. And that slowed them down so that they became easier targets than when they were galloping along the river bank.

'Cut 'em down, boys!' yelled Wade, and he shot another man out of the saddle, brought down a plunging horse that threw its rider who struck out frantically for the bank. The relief driver in the rear of the wagon picked him off just as he climbed out and the man fell backwards and sank.

Even so, the raiders were still riding the current down on to the wagons, pouring in the gunfire. Then Wade saw the first wagon floundering up on to the far bank and, as soon as it was safely on dry land, the driver locked on the brake, wound the reins around the lever, and jumped down, shotgun in hand. The Greener thundered and sheets of buckshot tore the water; one of the raiders lost most of his face.

The second wagon would be in the shallows very soon now and Wade swung away to lend a hand with the third, which was not only lagging behind but had slid its rear wheels off the slimy rocks so that one corner was awash.

Matthew Wade was surprised to see that one of the freighters under the canopy was struggling to heave a cask over the tailboard. Even as he watched the man managed it and the cask bobbed away on the sluggish current. But the man had turned back and was in the act of heaving a second cask over the rear of the wagon. Another man crouched in there, too, and tossed out some of the bean- and coffee-sacks. All were carried away on the current, the first of the casks already rolling into the shallows of a curving sandbar.

'The hell d'you think you're doing?' Wade yelled, face streaming with sweat and muddy river-water, smudged with powder-smoke. He triggered at the attackers as he moved to the tailgate.

The man inside, Kellerman, a big Missouri farm boy who had himself a tubby *señorita* awaiting him in Monterrey, turned his congested face towards Wade, gave another barrel a final heave so that it splashed into the river, and then tried to grin as he panted his answer.

'Kendrick's — orders, Matt — said if we was — hit — to let 'em have the casks — with the tarred X marked on 'em.'

'That's right, Matt,' spoke up the other man, tossing a bag of beans into the river. 'Any bags or barrels or packages marked with an X we was to let the Injuns have. Slow 'em down, he reckoned.'

'Son of a bitch!' snapped Wade, reloading, ducking as bullets snapped through the taut canvas, splintered the tailgate. He hipped swiftly in saddle, threw the Winchester to his shoulder and felt the brass butt-plate jar against his muscles as he triggered and levered three rapid shots. A painted Indian went down in a lather of water, his horse stumbling and falling on top on him, pinning the man as it floundered in its efforts to rise. Another raider clawed at his bloody face and his horse veered, but he didn't fall although he swayed wildly in leather.

The third man's horse was hit and he dived bodily out of the saddle, jamming a knife between his teeth, swimming desperately towards Wade. The freight boss twisted about in the saddle, trying to knee his horse into a position where he could shoot the man. He fired wildly and then the Indian came surging up out of the water with a blood-chilling war-cry, slashing with his knife. The blade hacked into the horse's withers. The horse bucked and whinnied and Wade fell on top of the renegade.

The blade swung at him and he

jerked his head aside, sinking, but jabbing with the rifle. The barrel took the red man under the arch of his ribs and his breath gusted out in a muddy bubble. Wade pulled the trigger and the gun almost jumped from his hand. His ears felt as if they had been clapped between two trashbin lids.

Almost deafened, he surfaced through the bloody water and grabbed at the side of the wagon, which the driver had managed to get back on an even keel, whipping up the mule-team, moving it forward over the river-bottom stones with crunching sounds. His mount was swimming still, though bleeding, and Wade's ears were still ringing from the under-water shot. He kicked the Indian's body away as it bumped against him, hung on, heard the wheels grinding on sand and felt the angle change as the team hauled the wagon through the shallows and up the bank.

There was still gunfire, but when he dropped to the ground and, gasping and retching muddy water, looked back across the river, he saw the renegades were swarming about the casks and sacks and packages that had washed up. They were like children, laughing, rolling the barrels clear of the water, dragging the dripping sacks ashore, some taking time to send a few final shots after the freighters, but their hearts weren't in it now; they had what they wanted: *food*.

Matthew Wade took a head-count. Two men were dead and three wounded, one man seriously. Also one mule was dead, another hurt badly enough to be shot minutes later.

'All right, get the wagons checked over and rolling. We'll have to get Buck to a sawbones in Laredo as quickly as we can. Won't be for a couple of days, though.'

'Matt, I can ride on ahead and bring a doc back,' spoke up Waco Grimm, Buck's sidekick. 'I don't think them Injuns are gonna worry us no more now . . .'

Wade made a snap decision and told

Waco to take a spare mount from the small remuda that accompanied the wagons. The man lost no time in getting away.

Then Wade turned back to Kellerman.

'Tell me about Kendrick's orders.'

Kellerman's heavy face straightened and he looked sidelong at the other man who had helped him throw over the sacks and barrels. The man wouldn't meet his gaze and turned away, suddenly interested in examining the iron tyre on the nearside wagonwheel.

'Well, it was when we were loadin' in the warehouse in Christi, with the new stuff from the boat Matt. Kendrick come down and took me an' Stump over to a corner and showed us the casks marked with an X in tar, told us to load 'em on and make sure they was near the tailgate — and we was to toss 'em over the side if we was attacked — distract the Injuns he said. Reckoned they was old weevily stock an' it'd give 'em all a bellyache.' Kellerman grinned and some of the others who had gathered round to listen, smiled. 'Sounded like a good idea to me.'

Wade felt the man was telling the truth and might have left it at that, but Stump, coming back now from examining the wagon-tyre, figuring there wasn't going to be any trouble about dumping the goods, spoke up.

'Was more'n weevils gonna give them sons of bitches a bellyache.'

All eyes turned to him and Stump was suddenly nervous again, licked his lips as Matthew Wade's bleak green gaze settled on him.

'And what's that, Stump? Just what *is* gonna give the renegades a bellyache?'

Stump shuffled his feet. 'Well, I know a feller named Joe Rivers who does a leetle work around the warehouse in Christi when he's short of cash — He tol' me him an' another feller was paid double for mixin' that stuff they lace the coyote baits with into the flour casks and some bags of beans an' coffee. They had to mark everythin' with a big X so's it wouldn't get mixed up with the rest.'

There was dead silence now and Kellerman said in a husky voice that was touched with a little horror:

'Judas, man, that coyote bait is full of strychnine!'

'That's the stuff!' Stump agreed, looking worried now, though. 'Kendrick said he'd seen it tie them wild dogs into knots and he wished he could see it do the same to the Injuns.'

'Nits breed lice,' breathed Wade and the men looked at him. 'One of our better-known army generals made that observation just before his men rode in on an Indian encampment on the Washita with orders to kill 'em all, women, kids, everyone. Always figured I'd like to have met that general some dark and stormy night in a back alley . . . '

One man swallowed audibly. 'Hell, Matt! I got no damn use for Injuns, but — women and kids'll be eatin' that flour and beans! Mebbe I ain't worried too much about the squaws, 'cause they can be meaner'n the bucks but . . . well, I got kids of my own!'

'Yeah,' Wade breathed grimly. 'Kendrick'll be in Laredo by the time we get there. Reckon I'll look him up and see what he has to say.'

As the men moved away to get the wagons a'rolling again, more than one said, quietly,

'I'm sure as hell glad *my* name ain't Kendrick!'

2

Laredo Sundown

After Buck Searles had been taken to an infirmary — the young doctor who had accompanied Waco back to meet the freight-wagons had treated him on the spot but didn't hold out much hope of his complete recovery — Wade saw to the deliveries with the Rio Bravo's agent, gave the men an advance in cash and went looking for Steve Kendrick.

The agent, Al Sutcliffe, looked warily at Wade when he asked where he might find Kendrick.

'He was here, but I don't think his reason for bein' in Laredo is what you might call official, Matt.'

Sutcliffe was a beefy man, very wide in the shoulder so that he looked even shorter than his five feet six. He had a wall-eye and Wade had always figured the man had found this useful inasmuch it allowed him not to meet anyone's gaze straight on. He had been caught out a few times trying to smuggle contraband down to Monterrey but Marc Brennan had never made any attempt to fire him, mainly because Sutcliffe was something of a hotshot at finding freight to be moved so that it was rare for any of Rio Bravo's wagons to return empty.

'I don't care why he's here, Al, I just want to see him,' Wade told the man curtly. 'You know where I can find him or not?'

Sutcliffe narrowed his eyes, his heavy features seeming to tighten. But he was a man who had always gone out of his way to avoid tangling with Matthew Wade. It wasn't so much fear as respect for the big tough freight-boss.

'I dunno where he *is*, Matt,' he said carefully, 'but he was askin' after that Spanish schoolmarm — you know the one I mean? She fussed with us over the

delivery of some lace or somethin'
that'd been shipped in from Spain for
her . . . '

'I recollect,' Wade allowed. 'Where's
she hang out?'

Sutcliffe shrugged. 'I told Kendrick
to try the schoolhouse . . . '

'Sounds right.'

Wade left abruptly and made his way
through the hot and dusty town which
was enveloped in a thin haze turning
deep amber as the sun slid slowly
towards the west. Some of his men were
sitting on a saloon veranda, drinking,
and they raised their glasses to him,
called to come join them.

'Be along soon — save me a
whiskey-and-beer chaser.'

Townsfolk stared at him as he
shouted his reply, a couple giving him
unfriendly looks. Freight-men were
welcome only for the goods they
brought. Otherwise, they were looked
upon as no better than cowhands
looking for a wild time at the end of the
trail.

Wade was wearing his stained trail-clothes and his bullet-punctured hat, his worn and blackened chamois work-gloves on his hands, and his Colt on his right hip. When he paused to tie the thong that held the holster base against his thigh, folk gave him a wide berth. They correctly read in his tall, muscle-tensed frame and weathered lean face, the signs of impending trouble for someone.

But the trouble was all for Steve Kendrick, whom Wade found outside the small school-building, sitting in the shade of an elm tree, smoking one of his cheroots, his appaloosa mount standing patiently nearby with trailing reins.

Kendrick was a big man, three inches over six feet which gave him a couple of inches on Wade, and he had another thirty pounds packed on his large frame. It was all muscle and sinew and his face bore a few scars from past fights, but not many, because Kendrick rarely lost. His eyes were the colour of beer and they pinched down as he watched Matthew Wade striding towards him. He read trouble in the set of Wade's wide shoulders, his kind of springy walk as though he was all ready to start dodging fists, and in the way that right hand never strayed more than a couple of inches from the smooth cedar butt of the low-slung Colt.

Kendrick ground out the cheroot and stood lazily, though already tensing, as Wade stopped a few feet away.

'Howdy, Matt. Good trip?'

'Hit by renegades again.' Wade's voice was flat and his eyes drilled into Kendrick's rugged face. 'Kel and Stump made sure they got those specially-marked kegs and bags you told 'em to throw off the wagon.'

'Good. 'Bout time we showed them Injuns they can't just take what they feel like.'

'Brennan know the flour and beans and coffee were laced with strychnine?'

Kendrick's face straightened. 'Who told you that?'

'Never mind. Did Marc know about it?'

Kendrick shrugged. 'None of your business anyway, Matt. Your job is to deliver the goods.'

'Not grub laced with poison, not even to renegade Injuns! You ever consider that women and kids'll be eating stuff made with that grub?'

'Sure. That was the idea. Stop the bastards breedin' make things easier all round.'

'You lousy son of a bitch, Kendrick!'

The troubleshooter arched his thick eyebrows.

'Never knew you was an Injun-lover!'

'Kids are kids, goddamnit! The women don't ride with the men! And I wouldn't poison the men, either!'

Kendrick spat casually. 'Well, what you'd do and what I do — which is my *job*, I might add — are two different things. You got any complaints, you take 'em to Marc.'

'I may settle with Brennan later. Right now I'm here to settle with you.'

Steve Kendrick suddenly grinned, immediately took off his frock-coat and hat, his slicked-back black hair glinting in the westering sun. He folded the coat carefully and laid it on top of his hat under the tree.

Wade waited, gloved hands starting to curl into fists.

Then suddenly Kendrick spun around, left hand sweeping gravel and pieces of dead bark into Wade's face.

The freight-boss threw up an arm but a shade late and his eyes stung as he instinctively jerked his head to one side in a ducking motion. Before he could straighten again, Kendrick's big body smashed into him, large hands grasping his shirt and hurling him face first against the tree. The cloth ripped and Wade managed to get one hand in front of him to absorb some of the impact. Even so his nose crunched and squirted blood and he stumbled. Kendrick came striding, grabbed Wade by the back of the neck and brought up a knee with a grunt.

The force flung Wade back three feet, his boots tangled and he tripped and went down. Instinct made him roll as Kendrick leapt in, already stomping. He missed and the force of the blow jarred up his leg, making him stagger a little. Dazed, but a brawler from way back and so operating on instinct, Matthew Wade lifted his boots against the big man's shins. Kendrick yelled as the spurs raked his flesh and shredded his trousers. He reached down quickly and Wade came up off the ground as if driven by an uncoiling spring. The top of his head smashed into Kendrick's face and the man hurtled back, arms flailing. He staggered and stumbled in his efforts to keep his balance but he went down, one hand reaching to keep him from sprawling all the way.

Wade came for him, fists cocked, bloody-faced, eyes alert, walking with that peculiar springy step. Steve tried to scoop up more dirt to throw in his face but Wade stomped on his hand and the big man grimaced as he grunted in pain. A boot skidded alongside his jaw and he thought his head was coming loose from his shoulders as he rolled over and over down the slope towards the main drag of Laredo.

A few men had already seen the fight up on the slight rise near the schoolhouse and they shouted to others so that by the time the two brawlers reached the street proper there was a small crowd, with men jostling for position, yelling, rooting for one man or the other without knowing anything much about them or the cause of the fight.

Laredo needed something to liven it up, they reckoned, something like a good fight . . .

Well, they sure got it.

Kendrick somersaulted over a hitch rail and the two mounts tethered there dragged at their reins and whinnied, rearing back. One got free and ran wild, scattering the crowd. Some men cussed, others, with drinks or bottles in their hands, laughed and cheered.

Kendrick wasn't cheering, though, as he picked himself up, tore a loose plank from the boardwalk and swung at Wade's head as he came in. Wade ducked and Kendrick stumbled, off balance from the swing with the heavy plank. The man righted quickly though, held the plank like a lance and ran at Wade who wasn't quite fast enough to leap aside. The edge of the plank, with a bent nail protruding, hooked into his shirt, stopped his movement abruptly, and tugged him off balance. His body swung back, right into the path of the plank-end. It cracked solidly against his ribs and he was knocked backwards. Kendrick bared his teeth through bloody and split lips, hefted the weapon again and rammed once more into Wade's body.

The freight-boss went down on to one knee and only just managed to drop his head under the wood as it grazed his skull, taking some of his long hair with it. Dazed, and still struggling to get up, Matthew Wade wiped blood out of his eyes, fell, then got his legs properly under him. As Kendrick charged in again, roaring, the plank aimed directly at his face now, Wade went low and dived for the man's thick legs. His shoulder rammed against Kendrick's knees and the jar halted the man abruptly. The plank tilted to one side as it broke from his grip and before he could right it, Wade reared up inside his thick arms, battered them aside and banged his head under Kendrick's blood-dripping chin.

The plank fell with a heavy, dull thud and Steve Kendrick lurched out into the street, trying to stay on his feet. The crowd roared as Wade went after him, stalking the man, driving him backwards with heavy blows, first a right, then a left, then three more lefts jerking Kendrick's head violently on his shoulders, followed by a hissing right that put the man down in the dust.

Wade spread his feet, hands hanging, gloves spattered with blood and little bits of flesh, gasping for breath as

Kendrick rolled about. But the big man shook his head angrily and with a roar surged upright, rushed Wade and pummelled him with a barrage of blows, each driven by powerful shoulder-muscles added to the weight of his arms.

Wade was hurled back into the crowd and they yelled and cheered as rough hands grabbed at him and threw him back to meet Kendrick's onrushing charge. Wade stepped to one side, thrust out a leg and this time it was Kendrick who rammed into the crowd, taking seven or eight men down with him, the others laughing and kicking just for the hell of it.

They threw him back and Wade was waiting, fists cocked. His gloves made mushy sounds as they pounded Steve's bloody face, turning the big head brutally. Wade shifted his attack to the midriff and while the first couple of blows made Kendrick gag and start to double over, the man tensed his washboard midriff and was unaffected by the next barrage of blows.

He bared those big teeth again, thrust out a hand and twisted it in Wade's long hair, yanking the man painfully off balance. He tried to knee Wade in the groin but the freight-boss was at the wrong angle. Even so, Kendrick's hard knee made Wade's leg buckle and the pain ran clear across his belly and up into his hip. Sagging, trying to stand upright, Wade took a bunch of knuckles on his left ear and his head rang wildly so that the crowd's shouting faded into a kind of distant buzz. Then he was lifted bodily by the torn shirt-front and hurled on to the boardwalk.

Men got out of the way quickly as Kendrick strode after him and stomped at his face with his riding-boots.

The crowd was suddenly silent. Fun-time was over — it had finally penetrated their alcoholic fog that this was no punch-bag, light-hearted brawl: this was a mean knock-down drag-out fight and the loser would be lucky if he ever got to use all his faculties again.

They watched quietly as Kendrick stumbled when Wade caught the down-driving boot, twisted savagely and rose off the boardwalk at the same time. Kendrick went through a plate-glass window displaying ladies' hats and gloves and button-up boots. The falling glass shards kept the crowd back and Kendrick was cut badly, his clothes torn, but as Wade stepped in to haul the man out of the display area, glass crunching underfoot, Steve lifted both legs and drove his boots against Wade's chest. The freighter staggered back off the edge of the walk and put down a hand to keep from falling all the way.

Covered in blood, clothes hanging from his upper body in shreds, big Steve Kendrick made an awesome figure as he elbowed and jostled the crowd aside and stormed after Wade. He jumped from the walk and his big body bore Wade to the ground. Kendrick swiftly straddled the man and locked his blood slippery hands around Wade's throat, squeezing as he cursed, bloody spittle flying, eyes bulging in their wild hatred.

It was clear he meant to kill Wade.

The freighter-boss writhed and tore at the iron-hard wrists as the breath was slowly squeezed out of him, throat closing, chest heaving as fiery clamps seemed to tighten remorselessly about his lungs. His head was roaring and his vision was going red, fading rapidly, and he knew he was going to die here in the filth of a Laredo gutter.

That knowledge saved him. It sent one last burst of electric energy through him and he snatched his Colt from his holster and smashed it violently across Kendrick's head.

The big man reared up, his eyes so wide that some of the crowd thought they might pop out on his scarred cheeks.

'It ain't . . . ' he said clearly and then his eyes closed and he fell sideways, hands coming loose from Wade's throat. The freighter-boss kicked away and rolled on to his face, gagging, retching, spitting blood and a broken tooth.

The crowd stayed where they were for a short time, silent, then someone scooped a hatful of water from the horse trough and tipped it over Wade's head. He rolled on to his back, spitting and spluttering, blinked, and suddenly grinned through all the watery blood and grit and straw.

'*Gracias, amigo,*' he said, then fell back, gasping, closing his eyes against the ruddy glow of sundown. He sighed and his body went limp.

Three of the freighters, including Kellerman and Waco, stepped out of the crowd, a little bleary-eyed, but concerned for their battered boss.

Between them, they lifted his unconscious form and started to carry him back towards the old rooming-house on McAllen Street, which they always used when in Laredo.

As they took him in the side door, Kellerman calling for Mrs O'Shane the owner, the sun set over the border town, painting it with blood-red light.

Maybe it was a portent.

3

Border Run

'I want you out of town just as soon as you can sit a hoss!'

Sheriff Roy Engels was red in the face as he glared down at Matthew Wade where the battered freighter-boss sat on the edge of a narrow bed in his room at Mrs O'Shane's.

His face was bruised and misshapen, one eye half-closed. There were narrow strips of plaster holding closed a deep cut above that same eye and his nose was swollen. He wore a clean shirt but it hung open to the waist, revealing dark, boot-shaped bruises on his body.

'You're a troublemaker, Wade!' the sheriff continued, still angry. 'I've had cause before to haul you over the coals and you and your men've wrecked the saloon bar moren'n once.'

'This time I fought a son of a bitch who poisoned a bunch of hungry Injuns, so you're kicking me outta town?' Wade's words were slurred because of his swollen lips but that good eye was cold and angry. 'And the fact that the window Kellerman busted when he fell through it happened to be in your sister's drapery store has nothing to do with it, I suppose.'

The sheriff, a tall, lean, rail of a man with drooping frontier moustache, bent forward slightly from his narrow waist.

'Listen, Wade, I don't like you, never have. You get sassy with me and you'll find yourself behind bars!' He let that sink in and then allowed himself a half-smile. ''Sides, what's all the fuss? We've had our fill of Injun raids around here. A lotta folk figure that feedin' 'em poisoned grub was a damn good idea!'

Wade continued to hold the man's angry stare.

'How *is* Kendrick, by the bye? I hear the Spanish schoolmarm is taking care of him.'

Engels' face coloured more deeply.

'She's a kind woman.'

'You doing any good there? Last time I was here we had a run-in 'cause I danced with her at the hoe-down and you claimed she was your's for the night.'

Engels just managed to stop himself from hitting Wade. '*OK!* You wanna be a smart-mouth, do it someplace else! You got two hours to git outta town. Take your men with you.'

Wade stood a little unsteadily.

'They had nothing to do with this, Engels. I'll go to save more trouble, but you let them stay and relax some. We have to wait for freight going north, anyway.'

'Not if I say different. But, all right. Your men can wait.' He shook a long, bony finger in Wade's face. 'But,' he fumbled out a battered brass-case, turnip-watch and squinted at the face, 'you've got two hours, not a minute more. I find you here thirty seconds after eleven fifteen and you go into the cells.' He grinned crookedly. 'Just for the record, Judge Corliss has a soft spot for that Spanish 'marm, too. He ain't too happy that she's nursin' Kendrick.'

Laughing harshly, he left the room. Wade shook his aching head slowly, and began to button his shirt.

★ ★ ★

Waco Grimm and the others lounging around the veranda outside Mrs O'Shane's stared hard at Wade's warbag as the man came through the door, rifle over one shoulder.

'Movin' house?' Waco asked, voice gravelly; the whole bunch were hung-over and looked it.

Wade set down the bag and shook his head gently, told them about Roy Engels' ultimatum.

'Don't like it that the Spanish gal's looking after Kendrick. So, he had to take it out on someone. I was handy.'

'Hell, we'll come with you,' said

Stump. 'We can spend our pay some-place else, don't have to be in Laredo.'

Others agreed but Wade said 'no'.

'Al Sutcliffe says there's some goods due in from Mexico that'll fill two wagons, so you wait for them — should only be a couple of days. I'll pick you up along the trail.' He hefted the warbag again. 'I'll go see if Al's got something for me to load into number three wagon. Recollect seeing a shipping-list for Monterrey on his desk.'

The word *Monterrey* made Keller-man sit up and take notice.

'Hey, Matt — you'll need a sidekick. I'll come with you.'

It hurt Wade to smile but he managed it, knowing the big Missou-rian was thinking of his chubby *señorita* waiting for him — he hoped! — in Monterrey.

'OK, Kel. Try and stay out of trouble for a couple of hours. If Al has a freight load, we'll go together.'

Kellerman grinned widely and Stump, beside him, punched him

lightly on the shoulder. That started a good natured scuffle and the rest joined in, gradually making their noisy way out of McAllen Street on to Main — and heading for the saloon . . .

Al Sutcliffe's wall-eye was angled well away from Wade's face as he smiled slowly.

He said, 'Now that's a coincidence, Matt! I've got this urgent load to go down to Monterrey. 'Fact, was gonna ask you if you could make the run. Papers are all fixed for crossin' the border and you take the stuff straight to the owner, not our warehouse.'

Wade frowned. 'The hell is so urgent?'

Sutcliffe's grin widened, and when he spoke his voice was low and conspiratorial.

'Water!'

He laughed at Wade's startled look.

'Yep! We got us a load of drill parts. Señor Rodolfo Grijalva will rendezvous with you in the hills just outside of Santiago. He's gonna drill for water on his land, figures to turn it into a farm. Used to run hosses but got tired of the rebels comin' down outta the hills and stealin' him blind. So he's sellin' off the broncs and gonna irrigate. Heard about them artesian wells they dug south of the Pecos. It's a gamble but he's got plenty of money.'

'Never heard of him.' Wade sharpened his gaze. 'You on a bonus if we get those parts down there quick, Al?'

Sutcliffe looked offended.

'Now, Matt, that's uncalled for . . . '

'How much?'

Sutcliffe sobered, took his time replying.

'Just a small commission.'

Wade didn't like it, but he figured to pull something out of this. Brennan would get mighty redheaded if he just allowed Engels to boot him out of town, so he had to make it worth while and Sutcliffe's deal was all that was on offer. Of course, he could just go north and wait until the others came with two out of three wagons loaded, but that wasn't Brennan's idea of getting the job done.

'How come all the papers are already fixed?'

Al Sutcliffe spread his hands. 'Told you, the *señor* wants the drills in a hurry — you don't find water overnight, you know. Almost as hard as findin' oil at times. Sooner he gets started the better, I guess.'

'You've done business with him before?'

'Hell, yeah. Several times.'

'How come you haven't ever offered Rio Bravo the freight before?'

Sutcliffe exercised his wide shoulders once again.

'You've always had full loads when Rodolfo had stuff to move. I'm an agent, Matt. I don't deal with Brennan exclusively.'

Wade heaved a sigh. 'All right. You'll need to have it loaded and ready to roll by eleven o'clock.'

'Judas! What the hell?'

'Engels' deadline for me . . . '

'Oh, well, you'll be able to make the drive yourself. There's only ten cases of drills, and one or two of tools.'

'Kel Kellerman's coming as sidekick.'

Sutcliffe frowned but brightened and said he would have the wagon loaded on time.

★ ★ ★

He was as good as his word and at three minutes past eleven Wade and Kellerman drove along Main and headed for the border crossing. The other freighters had already taken on a load of rotgut border whiskey and cat-called and yelled ribald remarks to Kellerman in reference to his waiting *señorita*.

Roy Engels lounged in the doorway of the law-office, turnip-watch in one hand, shotgun in the other, staring deadpan at the lumbering Conestoga. Wade threw him a mocking salute from the brim of his trail-stained hat but the expression on the lawman's face didn't change.

Kellerman, his breath potent with fumes of the bar whiskey he had consumed, rubbed his big hands briskly together.

'Man, I can hardly wait till I get to see Rosita!'

Wade knew Rosita was far from faithful to the big Missouri boy and only hoped Kellerman wouldn't walk in on her while she was entertaining another *amante*.

The crossing of the border at the Mexican customs was easier than Wade would have thought. But when he saw the *agente de policia* wave away the usual underling and take the papers himself, he felt a lurch in his belly. The official, smartly dressed in his brown uniform, gave them a perfunctory salute, his hand barely brushing the shiny peak of his cap. He looked at the *americanos* carefully rather than at the papers, nodded briefly.

'We have met before, Señor Wade . . . This is not your usual run, eh? A single wagon bound for Santiago?'

'It's all there in the papers, *jefe*,' Wade said easily. 'Al Sutcliffe said he had . . . arranged . . . everything.'

The officer's dark eyes narrowed. He tapped the papers as he shuffled through them, walked slowly around the wagon, asking Kellerman to untie the flaps so he might inspect the load.

Wade couldn't put down the feeling that something was wrong here. *By God, if Sutcliffe was using him for one of his contraband deals . . .* But then, if he was, and Wade was caught, there wouldn't be anything he could do about Sutcliffe — not for a long, long time. Maybe never — it was mighty hard to survive in a Mexican prison — sometimes a *contrabandista* never got closer to prison than the bullet-scarred brick wall in the yard.

Drive carefully, *amigo*, the officer said as he handed the papers back to Wade, suddenly smiling. 'The trail you will follow can be . . . dangerous. There is rain in the south and mudslides. You understand?'

'I savvy, *jefe*. And, *gracias* . . . I'll give your regards to Sutcliffe.'

Wade wasn't quite sure why he said that but the smile vanished smartly.

★ ★ ★

They figured to make camp north of Ignacio and the customs man's information about the rain proved to be true. It hammered down and turned the trail to slippery mud. Wade made for high country above the streams and gulches, for he had seen these unseasonal rains before, flash-floods coming down and catching unwary travellers in the thundering wall of muddy water laced with bouncing boulders and uprooted trees.

The mule team strained, unhappy about moving through the slanting rain. The wheels were losing their grip and Kellerman got down, braced the slick iron tyres with rocks underneath them, leaned his big shoulder against the tailgate. But it was a losing battle. Wade wasn't high enough above the eroded arroyos for his liking. Then, when a rear wheel dropped into an unseen hole and remained there despite an hour's effort trying to lift and prise it out, he gave up.

'We'll make camp here, Kel. Gonna be a cold one, but we've got lots of room under the canopy so we'll at least sleep dry tonight.'

Kellerman lowered the tailgate so as to climb in the rear, grabbed the edge of one of the rain-slick cases, to heave himself up. His muddy boots slipped and he fell against the lone case, balanced at the very edge. He felt it moving, yelled wildly and instinctively clung more tightly as the whole kit-and-caboodle slid off the wet wood. His weight helped pull it past the point of balance and he fell backwards, dragging the case with him.

Wade heard the strangled cry and the sodden sound as both man and box hit the muddy trail. He swiftly clambered over the back of the driving-seat and the stacked boxes inside. He swore when he reached the rear of the Conestoga and looked down at Kellerman sprawled in the mud with the box resting across his thick chest. Only it didn't look quite so thick now . . .

He jumped down and strained to move the box off Kellerman, surprised that it wasn't heavier. But it had been heavy enough to crush the Missourian's chest and in the flashes of lightning, Wade saw the blood pouring from the slack mouth. He heaved the box aside with a mighty shove and heard the wood crack against a rock as he knelt on one knee and tried to move Kellerman.

The man screamed and Wade actually jumped back. It was a piercing scream, like that of a wounded puma or jaguar, and echoed through the downpour. He eased the man back, resting Kellerman's head on his punched-in hat after managing to get him underneath the tilted wagon.

'Sorry, Kel, need to look at you.'

Kellerman's eyes were wide with fear in the next flash of lightning and one big hand twisted in Wade's sodden shirt.

'T-tell — Rosie — I-I love . . . '

The man coughed a great gout of blood that sprayed over Wade. Kellerman sagged, breath rattling horribly in his throat. Wade settled down on his haunches, thumbed back his own hat and squeezed water from his face with one hand. The ribs had snapped and obviously pierced Kellerman's lungs, and probably his big heart as well.

'*Christ!*' Wade breathed, but it was more a brief prayer than an oath.

It was one hell of a struggle but he managed to get Kellerman's body into the rear of the wagon amongst the boxes, covered it with the man's slicker. Panting, he sat down on one of the long boxes, wiped his nose on his sleeve, and stared unfocused through the gap in the cover.

He would have to take Kellerman into Ignacio. Well, that was the thing to do but he couldn't do it until daylight — and until he managed to get this damn wagon moving again. He would have to lighten it, but he didn't know if he could handle those boxes by himself. Kellerman could have ... *Quit that! Kel's gone and you're on your own ... If it has to be done, you have to do it ...*

He looked towards the fallen box just as lightning sizzled and crackled, lighting up the rugged countryside, sheening off the boulders and mud-slick slopes, revealing the few stunted trees whipping in the wind ...

And something else!

No wonder the box hadn't felt as heavy as he figured it should if it was stuffed with long lengths of steel drill.

The lightning flash clearly showed where the box had broken against a rock and the splintered wood had fallen away. The rain had battered open the tarred wrapping paper to reveal the contents.

From where he sat he saw clearly the

dark wood and gleaming metal of several rifles.

Wade swore, jumped down, slipped in the mud, fell across one corner of the box and gasped at the pain. He clawed his way forward, waiting for the next lightning bolt, but, perversely, it didn't come. The rain hammered down and the wind howled and battered at him but it was now as black as the workface of a coal mine.

Angrily, he groped in the tackle box under the seat, found the storm lantern, leaned under the canvas cover and got it lit. He turned up the wick, ignoring the pungent smoke and fumes, stumbled back to the broken box.

He fell several times, crawled to the box and stood the lantern on one of the unbroken planks. They were rifles all right, no argument there.

'Goddamn you, Sutcliffe!' he swore as he reached in and wrenched and struggled to get one free. It came, the others falling with a dull clatter, and he held it in the feeble light of the storm-lantern.

A Trapdoor Springfield — ex-army. And a long time 'ex', too, judging by the condition of the action. Everything was sloppy and worn. No doubt the firing-pin would be, too . . .

Then he heard the riders.

He snapped his head up, realized he had been hearing the sounds of hoofs for a minute or so above the pounding rain but had been so involved in the firearms, that it hadn't fully registered.

Too late, he lifted the hot smoky glass and blew out the lantern. Rain drops hissed against the chimney before it broke when it fell off the box. By then Wade was moving, slipping and sliding towards the driver's seat, clinging awkwardly to the wagon side as he reached up and snatched his rifle from under the seat. It was wet and he almost dropped it as he thrust away and started up the slope, boots sliding in the mud.

Someone downslope yelled. Another

voice took up the cry. Then several guns crashed and he heard bullets driving into the wet slope above him.

'*Alto! Alto!*' cried a voice clearly but Wade had no intention of stopping.

He clawed at the slippery slope, bent double, using his free hand as well as digging in as best he could with his boot-toes. He was fighting a losing battle and heard the clink of harness, the curses of men as they urged grunting mounts up the slope. The guns crashed again — he figured there were at least five or six — and the bullets spattered him with mud. He didn't shoot back: he was more interested in getting out of range or under cover.

If they were *rurales* down there his future looked pretty damn grim: his last view of this life would be through a stinking blindfold before the command to *Fire!*

He thought he was going to make it at first, but then he fell hard and his head rapped against a half-buried rock. He saw lightning-flashes this time, only they were inside his head and not tearing at the black night sky. He lost his grip on his rifle and then he was sliding back down the slope, incapable of stopping.

He landed in a crumpled heap on a reasonably level section of trail. Then the horses were gathered around him and saddle-leather creaked as men dismounted. A boot thudded into his ribs.

'On your feet, *amigo*!' a hard voice said, speaking American. 'And do it slow and careful or your head's gonna be rollin' on down the slope without you!'

Gun-hammers cocked and the dazed, mud spattered Matthew Wade clambered slowly to his feet, swaying a little, as he lifted his hands shoulder high and turned to face his captors.

4

Raw Deal

Suddenly he was squinting against a blinding silver white light that flickered over the drenched countryside, back-lighting the swollen leaden clouds high above.

During the flare, while squinting instinctively, he saw only too clearly who had captured him.

Rurales!

Leastways, there was a squad of them, maybe ten or a dozen, sitting their horses in their glistening slickers, brown peaked caps fastened by the chin-straps. They all held Mauser bolt-action carbines and all of the guns were pointed at him.

But there were others: Mexican *vaqueros* and a *jefe* off to one side sitting astride a big black Arab stallion that pawed at the mud.

And one more man.

The one who had kicked him in the ribs and now held a double-barrelled shotgun on him. The American. Shapeless in a slicker, but it couldn't disguise wide shoulders and the height of the man, which was about the same as Wade's. He wore a begrimed hat with the crown creased fore and aft, the rain pooling in it now and running from the stiff brim like a miniature waterfall.

The light flickered back to darkness before Wade could see the features plainly but he glimpsed the largish hawk-like nose, the wide, thin-lipped mouth, and the heavy brows that threw his eye sockets into black pools.

And there was only one man he knew who could stand hipshot while covering you with a cocked shotgun and still seem absolutely ready — and willing — to blow you in two if he figured it necessary.

'That surely ain't you, Rocky!' Wade

gritted and he saw the man stiffen slightly.

'Who's that?'

'Yeah, it's you. I'd recognize that Southern-fried accent anywhere! Last time I heard it you were calling out *Adios!*, high-tailing it on my bronc, leaving me standing in the middle of the trail like a damn statue while the posse rode in, swinging a lynch rope!'

The big man in the slicker leaned forward a little.

'No!' he breathed. 'Can't be you, Matt! Can't be!'

'It's me, you damn hoss-thief! And I've still got the ropeburn from that lynch-party's noose round my neck!'

'Hell, sorry about that, *amigo*, but you know the old deal we had. It was my turn to make the run for it, your turn to stay behind and give your pard a chance.'

'You got that deal all cockeyed, Rocky — it was only one of us to stay behind if there was no other choice, but that big buckskin could've carried both of us . . . '

'Not at the speed I needed him to go!'

Wade laughed despite himself. 'You son of a bitch! You haven't changed!'

'Uh-uh, Matt — don't move yet!' The shotgun's barrels jerked and Wade froze in mid-step. The man called Rocky turned his head slightly towards the watching horsemen.

'Sorry, Don Diego. Old pard, fallen on hard times it seems. His name's Matthew Wade.'

'And he, too, is a horse-thief?' asked the Mexican on the Arab mildly.

Rocky grinned, teeth flashing dully through the rain.

'That was a long time ago, Don Diego — I've been a good boy for years.'

'Not so your *amigo*, it would seem.' Diego heeled the big stallion forward and came up beside Rocky. 'Introduce me to your friend, Roca.'

'Matt, meet Don Diego Corzo, owner

of the Rancho Heroico west of Sabina. Mebbe you've heard of him?'

'Maybe I have,' Wade said slowly, still with hands raised as he inclined his head slightly. 'I wish we had met under other circumstances, Don Diego.'

The Mexican laughed, his teeth showing very white. 'I am sure you do, Señor Wade . . . But perhaps you have an explanation of how we have caught you smuggling guns to the *revolutionarios*? Perhaps you can convince us all that you are — innocent?'

'I'd sure like to try, Don Diego.'

Rocky Calloway remained silent, his face blank as Wade swung his gaze to the man. No help there!

Don Diego spoke quietly to one of his men, who dismounted immediately and went to the rear of the wagon. In moments he reported on Kellerman's body amongst the stacked boxes.

The Mexican looked sharply at Wade. 'It would seem that you have a great deal of explaining to do, *señor* . . . So perhaps we should all make our way to

Ignacio and more comfortable surroundings, eh?'

Wade thought the only 'surroundings' he could hope for if they got him to Ignacio was a cold stone cell with the *rurales* using him to break the monotony of a long, wet boring night.

'If I can get to my warbag in the wagon, Don Diego, I can show you papers that prove I work for the Rio Bravo Freight Company in San Antonio. My boss is Marc Brennan.'

'Ah! Now that is a name I know. Very well, Señor Wade, you, me and Roca will go into the wagon. My men are used to camping in all kinds of weather and I am sure that Teniente Gomez and his men have come prepared for rain or tempest.'

It didn't really mattter whether the *rurales* were prepared or not; a suggestion from Don Diego was the same as an order and Wade made a note of the way the lieutenant tossed off a snappy salute and growled orders at his men who started looking for shelter amongst the rocks.

Settled in the back of the wagon with a lantern burning, its mild heat causing steam to rise from the slickers and Wade's sodden clothes, he saw that Don Diego had steel-grey sideburns and a trim moustache. He looked healthy like most of the old *hidalgos* and while his features were hawklike and pleasant, the dark eyes were penetrating and seemed to look right inside a man. Rocky Calloway looked a little older but not as old as the number of years that had passed since last he and Wade had met. He had lank black hair that fell across his narrow forehead. He still had his good looks and Wade figured he would not be lonesome on Don Diego's *rancho*. Sabina was noted for its beautiful *señoritas* and Rocky had never been the shy type.

Automatically, Wade's gaze dropped to Rocky's left hip as the man shed his slicker. Yes, the gun was still slung the same way: high, holster slanted to the right, butt angled for the cross-draw that Rocky Calloway had always favoured. The man saw the direction of Wade's gaze and smiled thinly, pushing his wet hair back from his face.

'How fast are you these days, Matt?'

Wade raised his eyes to the man's face.

'Haven't had to worry about that for a long time.'

Rocky arched dark eyebrows.

'You don't practise?'

Wade shook his head. 'If it calls for shooting, these days I mostly use a rifle. Riding a freightline isn't like the old days.'

'Ah, the old days!' said Don Diego in his smooth voice. 'Yes, you both must tell me about them sometime. I am always interested when old friends meet after many years have passed — I am correct in saying you were once . . . amigos?'

'That's right, Don Diego,' Rocky answered quickly. 'Long time ago. Shared many a wilderness camp and the last plate of beans, and the last draw on a cigarette.'

'Hmmmm . . . Sounds like the life of an outlaw!'

'It was . . . exciting,' Wade admitted slowly, then dug out his papers and showed them to Don Diego who took a pair of folded, gold-wire framed spectacles from an inside jacket pocket. He set them on his dark beak of a nose and leaned towards the burning lamp, reading slowly.

'It would seem you are indeed a freight-boss for Señor Brennan, and have been for some years . . . ' The Mexican looked over the tops of the glasses. 'But I have never heard of the Rio Bravo line carrying guns for the rebels. Is this something new Brennan has started?'

Wade shook his head and explained how he had come to be driving the wagon-load of rifles.

'I was in a hurry to clear Laredo and figured this would be a fast trip and turn a little profit for Brennan. I ought to have stopped earlier to check out the boxes, but I'd heard there were rebels in the hills and I wanted to get through as quickly as I could.'

'It never occurred to you that any contraband you were carrying might be for the rebels?'

Wade met and held Don Diego's, unwavering gaze.

'No. I knew that Sutcliffe occasionally dealt in contraband but he'd never tried to put anything over on us — the freight-line, I mean. What he did was his own business as long as it didn't affect Rio Bravo . . .'

Don Diego said nothing, studied the papers some more, then asked for his *segundo* and Rocky Calloway bawled into the night. It was only moments before the Mexican who had earlier checked the back of the wagon appeared at the opening in the canopy. Don Diego spoke rapidly to him and the man hurried away. Wade started to speak but Don Diego held up a hand and they waited, listening to the rain pattering on the canvas. Wade thought it was easing a little.

The *segundo*, a man named Noah, appeared again and spoke quietly to Don Diego who nodded and waved him away. Then he turned to Wade.

'You realize you are in a great deal of trouble, Mateo?'

Wade frowned, gestured to the papers.

'I thought they explained my position, Don Diego.'

'They are genuine, I am sure, but . . . perhaps the quick profit you mentioned was to be more for yourself than Marc Brennan?'

Wade glanced at Rocky who was concentrating on rolling a cigarette with damp papers and tobacco.

'I don't go in for gun-running,' he said flatly and Don Diego frowned slightly at his tone, obviously not used to being spoken to like that. 'It happened the way I told you. If you don't believe me — well, I guess there's not much I can do about it. You've got

63

your *rurales* along and this is your country.'

'*Sí*, I have the upper hand and I am glad you realize it. It may make it easier for you to agree to what I am about to suggest . . . '

This time Calloway glanced up and although it might have been a trick of the flickering light, Wade thought he saw Rocky's left eyelid droop in a brief wink.

'I'm listening, Don Diego,' Wade said tautly.

'Good — Rancho Heroico is very large, almost as large as when my Castilian ancestors arrived in the days of the Aztecs and a man could claim land by the square mile. All the land taken in by a man riding a fast horse between sunrise and sundown was a typical claim.'

'Some Texas spreads were like that,' Calloway put in but neither the Mexican nor Wade commented.

'You were told you would be met at a certain place by this Rodolfo Grijalva,'

Don Diego continued. 'This man is also known as *El Tigre* — the tiger, leader of a very tough band of *revolucionarios* . . . .The *teniente* has agreed to my suggestion that you be allowed to keep this rendezvous. We will follow at a discreet distance and from there we will see where the guns are taken and it will lead us to the rebels' stronghold. You agree?'

Wade blew out his cheeks.

'Now hold on, *señor*. If this Grijalva is really a rebel, there's a good chance he won't pay up, except in lead. And you'll be too far away to be of any help to me.'

Don Diego smiled.

'Perhaps I did not make myself clear, Mateo — you either do this, or Teniente Gomez will take you to Ignacio and you will be charged with running contraband and as it is weapons for delivery to the rebels . . . ' He shrugged. 'I am afraid the mandatory penalty is death. You see your choice?'

Wade scowled. 'Plain as day! No

damn choice at all!'

Don Diego merely smiled.

* * *

The rain had stopped but the country-side was glistening with muddy patches and in several places there had been slides. Wade managed to work the big Conestoga around them and after travelling into the hills for a day and a half, he rested in the early afternoon to allow the mules a break. They had worked well but were now showing signs of restlessness and stubbornness and he knew from past experience that once the team was infected a man might as well go fishing while he waited for the mules to become more manage-able. Better to stop early before they became too rebellious. He rolled a cigarette and sat on a rock, smoking in the hot sunshine, studying the country he had travelled over.

It was fairly open, cut by dry washes and gulches and arroyos, with a few boulder-fields and two cuttings through low ridges. If Don Diego and his men were there — and he knew damn well they were — he couldn't see them. Not even a drifting haze of dust. No flash of light along a careless rifle-barrel or from the polished visor of a *rurale*'s cap.

Turning to study the country he had yet to enter chopped-up rocky ridges and baked slopes, mostly bare of vegetation — he couldn't see any sign of the rebels, either. They would have their look-outs, he knew, and their guards, but they were staying well hidden. Anyway, he wasn't due to reach the rendezvous point until tomorrow morning. But he would have felt better if he could have spotted *someone*, friend or foe, preferably friend . . .

Friend. *Amigo*. Pardner. That brought him to Rocky Calloway. Seven, no eight, years since they had separated on that mountain-pass trail in New Mexico, Rocky going hell for leather on the buckskin, Wade standing alone and on foot with only three shells in the rifle, plus one in the Colt.

And a bullet-gouge low in his left side, bleeding as he watched the dust-cloud of the posse coming closer.

He got under cover and actually had the posse's scout in his sights but he didn't pull the trigger. Hell, there was a lawman down there, leading them. So that meant no lynch party . . .

Boy was he wrong!

That badge he'd seen flashing in the sun was pinned to a temporary deputy - who just happened to be part-owner of the herd of horses Wade and Calloway had liberated from the working corrals of the mustang camp just below snowline in the sierras.

'That cottonwood yonder is a perfect gallows, men!' the damn deputy had said after they had the wounded Wade in manacles. 'Let's decorate it with this son of a bitch!'

Tired, dirty, hungry, missing their families after such a long chase, the posse were only too willing to get it finished and head for home.

They had the rope round his neck and were actually hauling him up, his toes just clear of the ground, when the real lawman, the town's sheriff, arrived with his part of the posse.

It saved his life and Wade made out he was hurt a lot worse than he was, so that the sheriff showed a little more humanity and allowed him to be confined in the town infirmary with an armed guard on duty. But the man cast an eye at the only nurse and was pleasantly surprised when she gave him back a smile that meant only one thing.

That night, while the nurse and guard were — er — occupied, Matthew Wade made his escape. He hadn't been near New Mexico since . . .

And until night before last he'd never heard what had happened to Rocky Calloway, either.

Now he knew. The man was trouble-shooter for Don Diego, wisely figuring that Mexico was safer for him than the good old U-nited States, and, according to Rocky, he had carved a neat little niche for himself on the Rancho Heroico.

'Home of Heroes,' Rocky had told him. 'That's what the Don calls it, but it was his grandfather or great-grandfather who named it that — got the place dotted here and there with armour and helmets and swords worn by his ancestors who came over with Cortez and the first conquistadores. Very patriotic, is the Don . . . that's why he's down on the rebels — and why they hit him whenever they figure they can get away with it.'

'Often?' Wade asked.

'Once is too often far as Don Diego is concerned but they've hit him mebbe a dozen times over the last couple of years. Wanted him to 'donate' to their 'cause'. Instead, he had Noah send back the man who'd come to ask tied across his saddle with an extra eye in his head.'

'Noah? That's the old Mex *segundo* with the thick gunmetal moustache?

Looks half-asleep most of the time?'

Calloway smiled crookedly. 'Yeah — *looks* that way. But did you also notice he wears two guns, very lowslung, and carries two knives — that you can see. I know he's got another in the top of each boot and one between his shoulders he can reach if someone gets the jump on him and tells him to lift his hands.'

'I'll remember that.'

'Don't bother, Matt. Just don't tangle with Noah at all. The word is he's killed thirty-some men and Don Diego only has to lift his little finger and he'll kill thirty more, go and confess in the chapel, come right out and do it all over again — if Don Diego says so.'

'Guess you mean he's loyal to Don Diego.'

'That's what I mean — and the Don hates the rebs. You dunno how lucky you are that I was there tonight. He could've had you shot where you stood. I've seen it happen.'

Wade poked at the small camp-fire with a stick. They were well away from the camp where the *rurales* had bedded down and out of earshot of the wagon where Diego and Noah slept — although Rocky said he didn't think that Noah ever slept, not until he was sure Don Diego was safe for the night, leastways.

'Rocky, why does Don Diego need you when he has a man like Noah?' Wade asked curiously.

Calloway's face was suddenly sober.

'I do special jobs for him — we get along fine — and like I said, you oughta think yourself lucky I saved your hide tonight.'

'Well. You kind of owed me that one.'

Calloway frowned. 'We gonna get in a hassle about that New Mexico deal? Not like you, Matt! Unless you've changed.'

'Guess maybe I have.'

Rocky snapped his fingers.

'Yeah! You said you don't practise

with your handgun no more. Hard to believe. You always did have a powerful killer-instinct, Matt.'

'Got it tied down, I guess. I was damn lucky not to be lynched and I lay low for a long time before I showed my nose in Texas. I get by OK now without drawing attention to myself by trying to be the fastest gun alive.'

Calloway shook his head. 'Never figured I'd hear you say that! Hell, you've lost all your ambition!'

Wade shook his head slowly. 'No. Just grew up.'

Calloway didn't seem to like Wade's implication.

He hadn't answered, smoked down his cigarette, then said curtly that he was turning in. Wade had the feeling the man was mad at him . . . but he wasn't about to lose any sleep over that. Not after all these years since they dissolved their partnership.

* * *

Now, on the hillside near the rebel rendezvous, Matthew Wade checked the loads in his Colt and Winchester and headed for the browsing mule-team; time to move on while there was still daylight and they were in a manageable mood. Shadows thickened quickly in these craggy hills . . .

★ ★ ★

That night, the mules hobbled, the wagon-wheels chocked, Wade turned in early, weary and still stiff and sore from his fight with Kendrick. He took his rifle under the blankets with him.

But it didn't do him any good.

He awoke sometime before midnight, judging by the position of the stars, to find he was surrounded by beard-shagged men in ragged clothes, all with weapons of some sort menacing him, ranging from razor-edged machetes to various types of rifles.

'*El Tigre* waits,' one man said and

kicked Wade hard in the side with a sandalled foot. 'Come now.'

Wade didn't see much sense in arguing, not against those kinds of odds.

5

Tiger's Den

They arrived just after daylight in the rebel camp.

Wade had seen nothing of the trail leading from where he had been captured. He had been tied hand and foot, blindfolded, and dumped in the rear of the wagon with the boxes. They had made no attempt to open the boxes but he had heard a couple discussing the one that had broken open on the rock during the rain a couple of nights ago. Wade and Don Diego's men had only been able to repair it roughly and their efforts were obvious.

When they arrived at the rebel hide-out there was a lot of yelling in Spanish and a couple of exuberant gunshots but immediately afterwards, even before the echoes had died amongst the iron-backed hills, there was an angry voice shouting abuse — apparently at the men who had fired the guns. Wade made out enough to savvy that someone in authority was berating them for wasting ammunition.

Then he was hauled roughly out of the wagon and stood upright while a knife sawed at his bonds. Horny nails scratched his face as the blindfold was torn off and he blinked in the early sunshine washing across the high slopes.

He glanced around, squinting, made out about thirty men — and a handful of women of varying ages — and the campsite in general. They lived in natural caves, it seemed, and there was an area where several cooking-fires burned, savoury food-smells making his belly rumble as breakfast was prepared. The men all looked wild-eyed and rough, their clothing mostly worn and patched or, in some cases, hanging in rags. Many were barefoot, but there were a lot of homemade sandals, too.

Except for one man: he wore dusty half-boots into which were tucked khaki riding britches. He wore a wide leather belt but had a revolver of foreign make carelessly rammed into it without a holster. His shirt was brown and sun-faded and his face was lean and hungry-looking, dark eyes giving Wade the once-over. There was a beard and a waxed moustache surrounding thin lips that had a cruel twist. He was neither very tall nor big, but there was something commanding about his presence.

'*Buenos dias, Señor El Tigre,*' Wade said quietly and a man nearby moved forward and struck him open-handed across the face.

'You will speak only when spoken to!' the man said in accented American.

Wade rubbed at the reddening mark on his face, his gaze bleak as he set it on the man who had hit him. By the voice, he knew it was the same one who had kicked him in the ribs at his camp.

'Your name?' snapped Rodolfo Grijalva, and Wade told him.

'Señor Sutcliffe has not used you before?'

'No. I had to leave Laredo quickly and also had need of extra *dinero*.'

El Tigre nodded, understanding well enough. The man next to him, the one who had struck Wade, spoke rapidly and quietly, gesturing to the rear of the wagons. The leader gave orders for the boxes to be unloaded and opened. 'We will eat.'

Wade followed the man to the cooking-fires and a young Mexican girl aged about twenty brought a plate of *frijoles* and corn with some kind of dark meat swimming in the spiced sauce. It woke him up and the girl smiled as he waved a hand in front of his open mouth, trying to cool it. She handed him a terracotta mug of water which he gulped gratefully, smiling back at her.

'Merida!' snapped Grijalva, and the girl gave a small jump. 'Bring me coffee!'

The girl obeyed at once and the Mexican watched Wade as he sipped the hot liquid.

'You have opened one of the boxes.'

Wade shook his head. 'An accident. It fell on to a rock.'

'You inspected the rifles?'

Wade hesitated. He shrugged. 'It was raining, so I covered them up quickly and managed to get the box back into the wagon.'

It was an indirect answer and it didn't please *El Tigre* but he said nothing more until they had finished eating and Merida took away their empty plates. At a sign from her *jefe* she brought Wade a cup of coffee.

There was some activity amongst the circle of rebel soldiers and Wade started when he saw two men being tied to wooden posts. They were stripped to the waist. He looked quizzically at The Tiger.

'They were foolish enough to waste ammunition. They must be disciplined.'

The man who had hit Wade — he

had heard Merida call him Juano — went to a pile of saddle gear and picked up a snake-like whip. He shook it out, cracked it around his head a couple of times, the plaited leather whistling through the air, then walked across to where the two men waited, tied to their posts. Their eyes bulged in utter terror.

Rodolfo Grijalva didn't even hitch around on his log to watch as Juano went to work, the lash cutting grisly patterns on the pale flesh of the men's backs. It seemed endless to Wade — the men were hanging in their bonds, unconscious — before The Tiger called casually, 'Enough.'

He stood and looked down unsmilingly at Wade.

'We will now test the rifles you have brought me.'

Wade's belly did a somersault. If all the guns were in as bad a condition as the Springfield he had seen . . .

'Whatever you say, *El Tigre*.' He tried to sound casual and followed the man across to where the boxes had been opened, their contents clearly seen in the brightening daylight.

Juano brought across a rifle selected at random and Wade groaned inwardly when he saw that it was an old Spencer repeater. *El Tigre* took it and examined it closely, seeming familiar with its operation. He glanced at Wade.

'Old! From your Civil War!'

Wade made a wide gesture with his hands.

'*El Tigre*, I am just a freighter. Sutcliffe had the boxes all ready to go . . . I know nothing about the guns or ammunition.'

He added the latter as Juano, tight-lipped, handed the man a battered tubular magazine for the Spencer. Wade could see the lead of the top cartridge; it was white with oxide, indicating age and possible unreliability.

El Tigre was not pleased but then he rammed the magazine into the butt of the Spencer and thrust the weapon at Wade.

'You will test-fire this gun.' He allowed himself the faintest of smiles. 'If that ancient ammunition blows up, at least I will not lose one of my men.'

Wade had no choice but to take the gun. He swore under his breath as he started to work the lever. It was stiff and the metal squeaked with lack of lubrication, but he jacked a shell into the breech and thumbed back the large hammer.

'Where do you want me to shoot?' he asked. Juano jabbed him with his own rifle-muzzle, a Snider with a rust-eroded foresight blade.

'You will speak with respect to our *jefe*!' he snapped.

Wade nodded. '*Perdone, El Tigre*,' he said.

Juano grabbed his arm, turned him roughly, pointing towards a thin clump of scraggly trees about forty yards away. Wade had his doubts about the old gun; he had seen the end of the bore and the rifling was badly worn. The wood of the butt and stock was cracked and dried out. There were flecks of rust on the barrel and action. The trigger felt loose.

He would be lucky if he didn't blow his head off.

'*Rapido! Rapido!*' hissed Juano. He lifted his whip which was still coiled and hit Wade across the side of the head.

Wade staggered. When he straightened up he swung the short Spencer rifle in a tight arc, slamming the rusty iron butt-plate against Juano's temple. The man's feet left the ground and he sprawled, barely conscious. Angry men started to close in and Wade turned his gaze towards Rodolfo Grijalva, prepared to take whatever punishment the man handed out; it would be worth it because it felt mighty good, smacking down Juano that way . . .

But *El Tigre* held up a hand and the men fell back, looking from their leader to the moaning Juano. They drew in sharp breaths as *El Tigre*'s right hand flashed across his body. Then there was a cocked pistol pointing at Wade. It had been done with the speed of a striking snake and Wade tensed, but even in his alarm he noted that the gun was a big English Webley — for some reason a popular handgun with Mexicans.

The barrel jerked slightly.

'Shoot at the trees, Señor Wade. Now!'

Wade slowly turned, lifted the rifle, pressing the butt firmly against his shoulder. He felt the slack in the loose trigger and wondered if there was even enough sear left to trip the firing-pin, but he felt the sudden pressure, then the abrupt let-off, almost catching him unawares. His breath was harsh in the back of his throat as he waited for the explosion that would take half his face off, embedding pieces of shrapnel from the erupted action in what was left of his skull.

It was anticlimax. The round misfired.

There was a murmur from the men but *El Tigre*'s face was impassive. The revolver barrel didn't waver a fraction as Wade ejected the dead cartridge and jacked another into the breech. This, too, was a misfire, as was the third.

But the fourth fired on cue. The Spencer kicked against Wade's shoulder and a piece of bark flew from a tree trunk, leaving a ragged white blaze. The men cheered — they were like children, enjoying seeing a bullet strike home.

The fact that it had struck a tree to the right of the one Wade had aimed at was not considered, and Wade sure didn't mention it.

But *El Tigre* was no fool. His Webley lifted briefly.

'Shoot at that tree with the big knot on the side. If you can, hit the knot.'

It was impossible, Wade knew, given the condition of the weapon and the state of the ammunition. But he tried to make allowances for the rifle, by aiming at the opposite side of the tree to the knot, and low. The next two cartridges misfired and that left only one in the magazine.

It fired and the bullet chewed bark

from the tree six inches above the knot. Wade thought it a pretty fair shot considering, but *El Tigre* was not pleased. As soon as his men saw that he was annoyed they began hurling abuse at Wade. Someone helped the dazed Juano to his feet and the man's eyes blazed hatred at the gringo as he picked up his whip and looked to Rodolfo for instructions.

He almost pleaded for a chance to whip the gringo.

'He will try other guns, other ammunition,' decreed the rebel leader and Wade groaned inwardly . . .

Half an hour later Wade knew he wasn't going to get out of there alive.

All the guns — Trapdoor Springfields, Spencers, even a few Zouave rifled muskets, battered old Henrys — were long past their prime. Actions were sloppy or jammed or simply refused to work. The ammunition's performance improved but there was little or no accuracy with any of the guns and Wade was only pleased that none had actually blown up, although several had cartridges jammed in their eroded breeches and he sure hoped The Tiger wasn't going to make him try to remove them . . .

Juano was hefting his whip expectantly. The Tiger had long since rammed his Webley revolver back into his belt. His face had been impassive through most of Wade's efforts but now he seemed to have reached the end of his patience. He wrenched the latest Henry that Wade had tested from the Texan's grip — the gun had performed dismally — and the Mexican smashed it savagely against a rock. He tossed the broken pieces at Wade's feet.

'Señor Sutcliffe has insulted me! Not only that, he has disrupted my plans! I cannot reach Sutcliffe, so I will have to send him something to show my displeasure.' The thin lips curled up at one side. 'I have decided it will be your head, Señor Wade.'

Juano's face split into a wide grin and he called to one of the soldiers to bring him his machete.

Wade had stiffened, surrounded by the press of the rebels as they poked and jabbed and jostled him, angry that their hopes of having new and reliable firearms had been dashed. Wade was the one within reach, and so he would suffer.

'Listen, *El Tigre*,' he said desperately as Juano tested the machete's edge with his dirty thumb, 'I had nothing to do with the guns — I just brought them here. Killing me won't change anything . . . '

'I think it will,' Grijalva growled. 'Sutcliffe is not so much of a fool that he will not see the warning when he receives your head. I believe he will realize his error and send me another shipment of guns, these in much better condition . . . ' He snapped his fingers and Wade was grabbed by eager hands.

He bucked and fought and butted and kicked but they forced him down to his knees and then pressure on his arm-sockets made him bend forward.

He flinched as the edge of the machete nicked the flesh on the back of his neck as Juano lined him up for the decapitating blow.

'Goddamn you, you greaser son of a bitch!' Wade gritted, straining to see *El Tigre*. 'I hope you rot in hell . . .'

'I am sure you will be there to greet me when I arrive, Señor Wade . . . Juano!'

Wade closed his eyes as Juano bared his teeth and swung up the machete, gripping it in both hands, rising to his toes so as to get full power behind the descending blade.

Matthew Wade thought; 'Damned if I ever figured I'd end up dying like this!'

And then there was a single whip-lashing, echoing shot followed almost instantly by the smack of lead penetrating flesh. There was a metallic clang as the machete fell to the parched ground in front of Wade's disbelieving eyes. Suddenly the grips eased on his arms as Juano's body sprawled across the machete, most of his face torn away, looking like a slab of newly butchered meat.

Then came pandemonium and volley after volley of gunfire. Rebels fell and writhed, some lay still, others ran for cover, shooting wildly down and across the slope.

Wade was free. As he started up a Mexican reeled into him and knocked him off his feet, pinning him by the legs, bleeding profusely from a neck wound. The Texan glimpsed *El Tigre*, with his huge pistol in his hand, shouting orders, spittle flying from his thin lips. The Tiger saw Wade and turned the Webley towards him, firing. The bullet thudded into the Mexican as Wade kicked free of the weight and snatched a pistol from the dead man's holster. He rolled away, another shot from the Webley gouging dirt and gravel as he twisted on to his back and chopped at the gun hammer with his left hand. There were three swift shots and Rodolfo Grijalva, alias *El Tigre*, reeled and shuddered with the strike of lead, his lean body crumpling to sprawl a bare yard from where Wade lay, smoking gun in hand.

The gringo snatched up the fallen Webley and with a pistol in each hand, thrust to his knees, seeing Don Diego and his *vaqueros* and the *rurales* thundering across the slopes, shooting and riding down upon the scattering rebels. But some of the Mexicans had dug in behind a barrier of stacked boulders near three caves that were closely linked, and he saw two of Diego's riders fall from their saddles.

'No *compasion*! No *compasion*!' shouted the *ranchero*, as he rode his big Arab stallion through a bunch of fleeing rebels, trampling three, shooting the other two with his pistol. Rocky Calloway was using his rifle, levering and triggering, shooting one of the running Mexican women as well as men in the group she was with. Noah had a pistol in each hand, blazing away steadily, always keeping his mount between any threat and Don Diego.

The *rurale* lieutenant, Gomez, had his sabre in one hand, slashing at rebels he caught up with, shooting his pistol from his other hand. His men were killing indiscriminately and Wade saw Merida running desperately, trying to escape two of the grinning *rurales* as they toyed with her, using their horses to push her this way and that, herding her towards some thorny thickets.

Wade triggered the Webley, bringing down one of the *rurale* mounts. The man was thrown heavily and skidded down the slope on his face. His companion had no idea where the shot had come from but he saw that the girl might escape now and he spurred his foam-flecked horse forward, raising his rifle preparing to smash in Merida's head.

Wade shot him out of the saddle. Then a bullet nicked the edge of his left ear and he felt the warm blood spray on to his neck. He whirled and fired at two rebels before the gun-hammers clicked on empty chambers. One man went down and the other ducked from sight.

Calloway rode in, Colt in hand now, leaning out of the saddle so he could see over the rocky barrier where rebels were resisting, and triggered until his gun was empty. He reined away, using his wild-eyed mount to head off a Mexican who was rushing at Wade with a machete. The man was hurled back two yards by the impact and Rocky reared his horse up on to its hind legs. The Mexican screamed as the forehoofs crushed his skull.

Wade leapt at a horse that was running by with an empty saddle; he had seen the rifle-butt protruding from the scabbard. He caught the mane. He lost the big Webley pistol but rammed the other into his belt. He felt his legs leave the ground, then he kicked up and strained with his arms, heaving himself on to the horse's back.

He settled, yanked the rifle out of its boot, levered, and felt a cartridge slide into the breech. He picked off three rebels before the remnants surrendered, standing up and shouting desperately, '*Renunciar! Darse por vencido!*' Giving up . . .

But if they expected mercy from Don Diego they were disappointed.

They were made to kneel in a long line and Noah walked behind them, shooting each in the base of the skull.

The slopes of the mountain were littered with dead men, by the far the most numerous being the bodies of *El Tigre's revolucionarios*.

Don Diego, face smudged with grime and powder-smoke, caught Wade's eye and he smiled.

'A good morning's work, I believe, *amigo! A muy bueno* morning's work!'

6

Payback

The wagon had been damaged during the fight and Don Diego's over-enthusiastic *vaqueros* set it afire, dancing around it and yelling as Merida and the surviving women brought them the remaining supply of the dead rebels' tequila and *pulque*. She expertly dodged grabbing hands, laughing.

There were plenty of spare horses and Wade chose a hardy-looking grey with a chiselled head and a wicked gleam in its eye. He figured he would need to make sure he was in control at all times but he could see speed and endurance in its muscled lines. Amongst the scattered weapons he located his own Colt and Winchester and felt more relaxed when he had them in his possession again.

Don Diego had made camp in a high cave that had obviously been used by *El Tigre*. He had Merida prepare a meal. He sent Rocky Calloway to fetch Wade and when they climbed back to the cave, Noah was standing guard at the entrance, face impassive as always, but his hard eyes followed Wade closely once he noted the man was armed.

The girl handed Wade a bowl of chili and a hunk of bread that he figured was at least a couple of days old and unleavened. But he was hungry, so he sat down on a rock and ate, watched by Diego and Rocky. The girl stood at his side.

'Come, stand by me, *señorita*,' said the Don. She hesitated, smiled down at Wade and moved across. Diego looked levelly at Wade. 'The spoils to the victor, eh, Mateo?'

Wade glanced up at the girl.

'Your right, I guess,' Wade said and saw the girl's face darken. Rocky noticed it, too, and made the expression on his face carefully blank.

'You prefer Señor Wade, eh, querida?' said the Don.

She flushed, looked at Wade from under her arched brows with her flashing dark eyes.

'He save my life — I go where he goes.'

Diego seemed amused. 'And what have you to say to that, Mateo?'

Wade swallowed the last of the bread he had used to mop up the chili in his bowl.

'You're a good cook — and good looker, Merida. But you can't go with me.'

Her face straightened. 'I *will* go with you! I am — good company.' She swept her arm about her, encompassing what could be seen of the battered camp through the entrance. 'These pigs kill my family, make me stay. Now I am go with you and make you happy.'

Wade frowned. 'I appreciate the offer, Merida, but I have things to do and I can't take you with me. But maybe Don

Diego could provide a good home for you.'

Rocky stiffened and Wade thought he heard breath between his teeth at his temerity in making such a suggestion to the Don. But Wade figured if Diego could put him on a spot then it was now his turn. The girl was stiff and straight-faced and her gaze narrowed as she watched Matthew Wade.

Don Diego suddenly smiled.

'Of course. It was my intention to do so all along. Come, *querida*, you will live at my *rancho*, and you will find happiness. Now you go and get what things you have and wait for me outside.'

The girl was clearly angry at Wade for his refusal, polite though he had tried to be, but she knew enough not to resist Don Diego. To refuse his offer could leave her in a mighty vulnerable, if not dangerous, position. There were plenty of those drunken *vaqueros* who would grab her if she did not already have Don Diego's brand on her.

She left sullenly, throwing Wade a narrowed, fiery look as she went.

'You have offended her, Mateo, but never mind that now. You fight well and Rocky has told me that you have worked for Brennan for some years, bringing freight all the way to Monterrey and beyond into the Sierra Madre. This is so?'

Wade nodded, accepting the tobacco sack that Rocky handed him, and commenced to roll a cigarette.

'We had deliveries in the Madre at times. I searched for Geronimo with the army there once but never found him.'

Don Diego nodded as if that was what he wanted to hear.

'Then it is clear you know the sierra well.'

Wade glanced at Rocky but the man remained silent.

Wade looked up and answered warily, 'Not as well as yourself, I think, Don Diego. I mean, you live close by and . . .'

He broke off as Don Diego waved a hand irritably.

'I have hunted there but prefer the Tamaulipas because of the greater variety of game. I have a proposition for you, Mateo. I am sure that Roca has told you that I pay well. I want you to lead me into the Sierra Madre, to a certain area close to north-west Zacatecas. If you hunted the Indian you mentioned, you must have spent time there.'

Wade lit his cigarette and nodded as he exhaled.

'I've been there. In fact, we spent weeks scouring that general area. But it's hell on earth, Don Diego — heat, and rocks and waterless, unpopulated except for *bandidos* and a mission at one of the villages — '

'Hardships can be overcome,' the Mexican cut in sharply and impatiently. 'Will you accept my offer?'

Wade deliberately refrained from looking at Calloway although he felt Rocky's eyes boring into him. He met

Don Diego's querying gaze steadily.

'Sorry, Don Diego. I have some unfinished business back in Laredo.'

'Agh!' the Mexican barked, making a sweeping motion with one hand. 'You mean Sutcliffe. Such a man is not worth turning down the money I can pay you just for a brief moment of revenge. I can send Noah if you wish.'

'You're missin' your big chance, amigo,' Rocky said quietly, but persuasively. 'Don Diego takes mighty good care of his own . . . '

Still Wade did not look at the gunfighter.

'I'm sorry, Don Diego. I do my own chores. I have to do this. I guess you might not savvy the way it is with me, but I've been wronged and I've never allowed that to happen when I was able to square things away. This is just something I have to do. And I aim to do it.'

The Don was silent, his face sober, his eyes shadowed by the brim of his hat. He took out a cigarillo. Rocky struck a vesta and held it for him. Don Diego glanced at Wade through the clouds of aromatic smoke.

'I understand how it can be with some men, Mateo — I should have seen that you are such a man. It is an admirable quality in any man but in this case it is also foolish. I can make you rich.'

'I've been there, Don Diego. Oh, not by your standards, I guess, but there was a time when Rocky and me had our own spread before certain people did us wrong and pushed us on to the owlhoot trail. It was satisfying, but I never did like the worry about how safe the money was and all the work involved keeping it that way.' He smiled crookedly at Rocky. 'And you left all of that side to me, you lazy sonuver!'

Rocky shrugged good naturedly.

'Those days are long gone, Matt. You're not much better off than a cowhand now. And Don Diego's offering you a chance you'll kick yourself hump-backed over if you pass it up . . . '

Wade stood up.

'I'm heading back to Laredo, gents. Maybe I'll come back this way with the next load of freight and maybe I'll be feeling restless or Brennan might not like what I'm gonna do to Sutcliffe, so . . . '

'The offer is now. If you refuse, there will not be a second chance, Mateo.' Diego spoke curtly, a little petulantly.

'Well, easy come, easy go,' said Wade and smiled but neither man seemed to think it funny.

Rocky followed him out of the cave, past the impassive Noah and down the slope to where Wade had left his grey tethered. Rocky caught him by the arm.

'Don't do this, Matt! Look, I'm tellin' you, this Sierra Madre thing could make you mighty rich.'

Wade frowned. 'How come? What's so important about the sierra?'

Rocky glanced around, making sure

they wouldn't be overheard. He spoke quietly.

'I've told you how Diego feels about his ancestors and so on. He's had part of an old map handed down by one of 'em that he says will lead to a lost Aztec treasure — a whole cave stuffed to the roof with gold hidden by the *conquistadores*. The Don wants — '

'Judas priest, Rocky! Not *you*! Not you falling for a lost-treasure yarn! Hell, the entire Gulf coast and all this part of Mexico is full of fast-talking *hombres* who are nothing but four-flushers and swindlers. I'm surprised that Don Diego would fall for such a thing.'

'You don't savvy! He didn't buy no treasure-map from some hocus-pocus down-and-out in a *cantina* with a dirt floor! This is a legacy! Somethin' handed down in his family for generations. Hell, he's even had me tryin' to locate the missin' part of the map. He *knows* the treasure's there, Matt! One of his ancestors hid it. He needs a damn good guide and I don't know no better one than you. Change your mind, *amigo*, I swear you'll be mighty glad you did!'

Wade shook his head, mounted easily and lifted the reins of the skittish horse.

'Not my line, Rocky. Look me up if you ever get back to the States. *Adios*!'

Rocky watched as Wade rode down-slope, and he swore.

It was only as he slogged his way back towards the cave where Don Diego waited talking with Noah, that he realized Wade hadn't said 'Adios, *amigo*!' as in the old days.

Just — *adios*.

★ ★ ★

Al Sutcliffe leapt up from behind his desk as the door of his office crashed open and Matthew Wade came in.

The big Texan looked almighty scary and dangerous, powdered as he was with alkali and reeking of camp-fire smoke and wild trails. He held his

Winchester in his left hand and his right hovered close to his holstered Colt as he strode across the small office towards the startled freight-agent.

'Wait up!' Sutcliffe cried hoarsely but, at the same time, he knew damn well nothing was going to stop Wade and with a small cry he lunged for his top desk-drawer. He had his hand inside, fingers wrapping about the butt of the sixgun that lay there on top of some papers when Wade rounded a corner of the desk and drove his foot solidly against the drawer.

Sutcliffe screamed as it smashed closed on his hand and wrist. He moaned sickly as he dragged the bleeding, torn member out and clutched it to his chest. Wade's rifle-butt drove into his mid-section and Al Sutcliffe doubled up, his legs buckling as he gagged. Wade flung him roughly into the desk chair with so much force that it all but tipped over. Wade steadied it, placed his rifle on the desk and one hand on each of the chair's arms, thrusting his beard-shagged, battered face close to Sutcliffe's as the man writhed, trying to get his breath.

'I'm back, Sutcliffe and I want answers!'

The agent coughed and tried to speak but Wade backhanded him brutally across the mouth. The man cupped his mouth with his hand as blood dribbled into it, together with a broken tooth. He looked up, eyes wide.

'Jesus Christ! Gimme a chance to . . . explain!'

Wade fisted up the man's shirt-front and shook him angrily, rapping the back of his head against the wall. Then he calmed down enough to step back a pace, placed his hands on his hips and glared down at Sutcliffe.

'I'm waiting, Al!'

Sutcliffe held up a shaking hand, trying to catch his breath, cautiously produced a kerchief and held it to his bleeding mouth.

'OK! We din' think it'd bother you

much runnin' a batch of guns but Steve said — '

'Kendrick?' Wade frowned as the agent nodded. 'What's he got to do with it?'

'Hell, Steve's been runnin' guns for some time. You've took 'em across before, mixed in with genuine freight — '

Wade swore. 'That son of a bitch!'

The agent waited, then, when Wade said no more, went on:

'Kendrick always comes down to smooth the way with customs at the border — you know, a handful of *pesos* in the right place — and also Roy Engels.'

'Judas priest! *Engels* was in on this, too? Seems like I'm the only one who wasn't!'

Sutcliffe shrugged. 'Best this way — the less you knew the better, but you had a real good rep as an honest freighter and had never been in trouble over carryin' contraband and we figured to use this to our advantage.

Look, Matt, it's a hard livin' workin' this border country and it was Steve's idea; you know what he's like at turnin' a fast buck . . . '

Wade stared down as the man's words trailed off. 'And you're just Mister Innocent.'

'Aw, Matt, I did my part, was all, Kendrick and Roy seen a chance to get these guns to Rodolfo quickly so he ordered you outta town an' I had the load ready. What went wrong?'

'You sons of bitches didn't count on a *ranchero* called Don Diego Corzo, did you?'

Al Sutcliffe groaned. 'Aw, hell, I knew he'd come down on us sooner or later! He's been raisin' hell with all the rebs down there! I'm sorry, Matt, gospel! I never knew you'd be headin' into any kinda trouble . . . '

'But you didn't warn me I might be, did you?' Wade gritted. 'And on top of that you sent junk guns that nearly cost me my neck — literally! I damn well ought to . . . '

He grabbed the blood-spotted shirt-front again and half hauled Sutcliffe out of the chair, his right fist drawn back. The agent abruptly came to life. From being nervous and scared he suddenly became a whirlwind of fists and boots, crowding the startled Wade back across the desk, throwing himself on top of the freighter, snatching up a bronze paper-weight in the form of a cowboy riding a bucking bronco, ready to smash it into Wade's bleeding face.

Matthew Wade brought up his knee. It caught Sutcliffe between the legs and the man sagged, gasping, the paper-weight thudding to the floor.

Wade came off the desk like a hurricane, fists pummelling the agent into the wall. He heaved him over the desk and the man sprawled on all fours on the floor, scattering papers and desk-top paraphernalia. He groaned and pushed upright, making a drunken, staggering run to the door which hung by one hinge.

Wade leapt over the desk, caught him

by the shoulder and spun him around, driving a fist into the bloody face.

Al Sutcliffe flailed backwards through the doorway and let out a strangled yell. He fell, clattering and rolling and banging and somersaulting down the stairs, splintering the support rails as he went. He landed in a huddled, bloody heap at the foot of the stairs, one leg at a strange angle, and the arm with the injured hand bent beneath his still body.

7

Jail

Merida had scrubbed up well, thought Rocky Calloway as he lazed in the shaded courtyard of Rancho Heroico, smoking, with a bottle of tequila on the table. He lounged back in the chair and watched the girl as she moved about the garden, collecting a basketful of flowers, cutting the roses carefully.

Don Diego had provided her with decent clothes and she wore a white-silk drawstring blouse and a swirling skirt of some lightweight material he didn't know the name of. Bands of coloured cloth at the base gave it weight so that when she walked it swung seductively between her long legs and showed off her young body.

Rocky smiled faintly. Trust the Don

to find something to hold a man's interest . . .

Since their return from *El Tigre*'s hide-out Diego had kept her close to him and he had given her chambers in the main house close to his own room: the same chambers that other women who had taken his eye were given when they came to stay a while at the hacienda.

She seemed happy enough in her new role and he figured she was sure being treated heaps better than when she had stayed with *El Tigre*.

'Hey, Merida,' he called quietly amongst the flowers. She glanced up. Her raven-black hair glinted in the sun and was tied with a red-and-yellow bandanna. '*Buenos dias*.'

'*Buenos dias*, Roca,' she said with a small smile. 'You enjoy the day, no?'

'I enjoy the day, *sí*!' he laughed, getting up to lean on the iron railing, at the same time looking to make sure that Don Diego was still down at the stables, watching the grooming of his

114

Arab stallion. 'You . . . enjoy the nights, too?'

The smile faded and she gave a small frown.

'Don Diego is kind.'

'But you've still just changed one man's bed for another, eh?'

She pouted and her skirts swirled as she turned away quickly.

'I do not like this talk!'

She bent over to reach a peach-coloured rose and Calloway admired the view appreciatively. He sipped some tequila and sucked a little lime-juice.

'Merida . . . you could leave.'

She glanced at him over her shoulder and took her time answering.

'This is good place. Best I have been since my parents were killed.'

'But you'd still like to leave, wouldn't you?'

She stared at him, frowning. 'You know you'll have to go sometime, when Don Diego says so. He won't keep you around for ever, Merida. He has lots of women. Besides, I saw the way you looked at Matthew Wade.'

She stiffened at mention of the Texan's name and her dark eyes flashed briefly.

Calloway laughed. 'Yeah! Like him best, don't you? Wouldn't care if he only had an adobe hut to offer, you'd rather be with him.'

She brandished the garden-shears at him, looking directly at the fork of his trousers, snipped the blades in silent threat. Rocky grinned.

'I just bet you would, too! Listen, Merida, Matt didn't want to leave you, but he had to. He told me when I was seein' him off. 'Rock,' he said, 'I surely don't want to leave that purty young *señorita* for Don Diego, but I figure it's best and safest for her. She'd be in danger if she came with me. I know I hurt her feelings, but it was the only way I could do it and be sure she'd be safe'.' Calloway shrugged. 'That's gospel, Merida. Matt just wanted what he figured was best for you.'

Her breasts were heaving with her

increased rate of breathing. Her eyes roved over his handsome face, time and again.

'This is — true?'

Rocky placed his right hand across his heart soberly.

'Swear it on my mother's grave, Merida . . . '

'Then I must go to him!' She looked around swiftly. 'But how? Don Diego would never allow!'

He tugged at an ear-lobe. 'N-noooo. But we don't have to have his permission.'

'*Estupido! Tonto!*' she hissed. 'He would send Noah!'

'Don't think so. Not if I laid a false trail to show we headed south — while all the time we was makin' for Laredo . . . and good ol' Matt.'

She was still uncertain but obviously wanted his words to be true.

'Very dangerous!'

'I can cut the odds. But listen, Merida, if we're gonna do this, you — er — have to do your part, too.'

Her look was wary, mouth tightening. 'What you want?'

'Just want you to do somethin' for me — no, no, nothin' like you're thinkin'. I'm not sayin' I wouldn't jump through hoops for you if you offered, but this is strictly business. You do what I want, and we take off for Laredo and Matthew Wade.'

'I — he *really* like me, Roca?'

'Hell, I been sayin' so, ain't I?'

'*Sí*, you say so . . . '

He smiled crookedly. 'Well, you're just gonna have to make up your mind whether you believe me or not, Merida. You don't want to come, then say so right now, before I tell you what it is I want you to do.'

Her face sharpened. 'Maybe — maybe I am *only* one who can do this thing you want, eh?'

He laughed. 'You're smarter'n you look, ain't you? But — no. I can do it myself, but it'll take me a lot longer. And I've waited long enough. I've got this hankerin' to go back to the good ol'

U-S again. So — you want to come with me or not? Just say . . . but say *rapido*. It's up to you.'

* * *

Wade had booked into his old room at Mrs O'Shane's, and the rough-tongued Irish woman had shaken her head at the way he looked: clothes trail-worn, spattered with fresh blood, his face still showing fading bruises from his fight with Kendrick, and now some new cuts had been added.

'Ah, 'tis the infirmary you should be bookin' into, Matthew Wade!' She tut-tutted and sighed. 'I'll be fetchin' you a bowl of warm water and some iodine and old rags, but you'll have to be doin' your own doctorin'.'

'Obliged, Mrs O'Shane,' he said, shouldering his warbag, rifle in his other hand, the skinned knuckles showing plainly. 'I'll clean up any mess I make.'

'That you will,' she said tersely and

went back into her big kitchen.

An hour later, Wade was cleaned up and more or less presentable, wearing a clean, faded, though wrinkled blue shirt. He had brushed some of the alkali and grease and dirt from his hat and trousers and dusted off his boots. His gunrig had been rubbed over with neatsfoot oil and gleamed dully; the Colt was fully loaded.

He asked Mrs O'Shane for some more hot water. She obliged and he soaked his aching hands in it before going out onto the street.

In the saloon he saw Steven Kendrick; the man happened to glance up from his beer at the same time and he stood abruptly. The dance-hall girl sitting close to him was almost knocked out of her chair.

'Take it easy, Stevie! We can go upstairs it you want . . .'

He slapped some money on the table and turned away without a word, hurrying out through the side door. Wade paused, then shrugged, and went back to his drink. He would settle with Kendrick later. Right now he was too weary and muscle-sore to get involved in another fight. A few drinks, maybe a little female company, and then he would hit the hay . . .

That was the way he planned his evening and also the way it went. But with one unplanned part: he had just taken off his gunbelt and hung it over the back of the bedside chair when there was the rap of hard knuckles on his door.

He had had quite a few drinks and had stumbled coming up the stairs, clattering a little. He figured Mrs O'Shane was about to complain.

'Sorry, Mrs O'Shane,' he said as he started for the door. 'Heel on my shoe is kind of busted and I slipped . . . '

He opened the door and froze — staring down the twin muzzles of a shotgun. It was held in the hands of hard-faced Roy Engels. Steve Kendrick was standing beside the sheriff, looking kind of smug, a crooked smile on his face.

'I'd say you were more drunk than fightin' a busted shoe-heel, Matt!' Kendrick said with a harsh laugh.

Wade said nothing, hand still on the doorknob. The sheriff backed him up into the room and Kendrick came in, closing the door behind him. The gun-barrels jerked and Wade, fast sobering, raised his hands shoulder-high.

'You been back in town only a few hours and you been in a fight already,' Engels said, stony-faced. When Wade said nothing, the sheriff added, 'With Al Sutcliffe.'

'And he complained to you?' Wade said scathingly. 'Ought to've figured that.' He flicked bleak eyes to Kendrick who still seemed mighty pleased with himself. 'His pard's in the gun-running deal.'

Roy Engel's face didn't change but his eyes narrowed dangerously and his knuckle whitened on his trigger-finger.

'That's your word agin ours, Matt,' Kendrick said cockily.

'Sutcliffe talked once, he can be made to talk again — this time in a court of law.'

Engels snorted. 'I can guarantee that won't happen!'

'Don't be too sure.' But Wade frowned. There was something in the lawman's tone — and Kendrick's attitude — that put a cold lump in his belly. They were too damn cocky and complacent ... What the hell had happened?

'Oh, we're sure, Matt, mighty sure!' crowed Kendrick. 'Dead men can't talk.'

Wade went very still. His mouth was dry and the rotgut he had consumed was suddenly sour in his belly. He flicked his eyes from one man to the other.

'Al Sutcliffe was still alive last time I saw him,' the freighter said slowly. 'Beat-up some, lying at the bottom of the stairs that lead up to his office, but he was breathing and cussing me when I left.'

'Yeah? Well, Al was found dead less than half an hour ago. Sprawled in his chair at his desk with his neck snapped.'

Wade remained silent for a long minute.

'He was alive, when I left him — a couple of hours back. He had what looked like a busted leg and arm. I doubt he could've crawled back upstairs.'

'Oh, reckon we could find enough sign to say he done just that,' Roy Engels said. 'If we try hard enough — eh, Steve?'

'Sure of it, Roy.' Kendrick leaned forward a little from the waist. 'You should've stayed south of the border, Matt. You're in more trouble than you can shake a stick at now.'

'You sons of bitches! You set it up!'

'You can tell that to the judge,' the sheriff said. He poked Wade roughly in the midriff with the shotgun. 'Now get your hat — I got a nice hard bunk in a draughty cell all ready and waitin' for you, Wade!'

* * *

When Roy Engels brought him his breakfast next morning, Wade took the tray through the special gap in the cell bars and asked,

'How long you gonna keep me here, Engels? You know damn well I never killed Sutcliffe.'

'I know what the evidence shows. You come back a'ragin', an' there's plenty folks seen the way you quit that grey you was forkin' at the hitch rail outside Al's office-buildin', plenty who'll testify how you stormed in like you was ready to kill, just like when you beat up Steve.'

Wade swore softly. He knew how he had been raging when he had returned to Laredo.

'If there were so many folk about, must've been some seen me leave Sutcliffe at the foot of his stairs — and take my hoss to the livery, too . . . '

Engels shook his head. 'Nope. Queer, ain't it?'

'Not so queer — my guess is you never asked anyone if they saw me leave.'

'Or mebbe it was gettin' on supper time and there just weren't no folk on the street who took notice.' The sheriff thrust his face close to the bars. 'Get used to the idea, Wade — you're gonna hang for Al's murder. An' there ain't nothin' you can do to stop it . . . unless you choke on your breakfast!'

The lawman went on back down the passage, chuckling. Wade carried his food-tray back to his bunk. He had suddenly lost his appettite.

It really did look as if they planned to hang him one way or another . . .

★ ★ ★

It was a long day. A couple of hard-faced deputies looked into his cell. One of them offered him a tobacco-sack and papers and lit the cigarette for him, but apart from saying that Al Sutcliffe would be no loss to the world, he showed no further interest in Wade. He left him his lunch and walked back down the passage.

Kendrick came in once to gloat, still smarting, obviously, from the battering he had taken at Wade's hands.

'This the only way you could get back at me, Steve?' taunted Wade, and Kendrick scowled and coloured so that Wade knew he was close to the mark. 'Gutless son of a bitch.'

'That so?' sneered Kendrick. 'See how smart your mouth is when they swing you from the gallows — we've got it all fixed. You're a dead man, Wade! Now, whyn't you lie down and relax. Have yourself a nice restful sleep . . . '

Kendrick went out laughing and Wade swore softly. He damn well had to get out of here.

And fast . . .

★ ★ ★

But despite the turmoil of his thoughts he dozed, and must have slept through delivery of his supper because it was cold and uninviting when he awoke and dark enough so that he knew it was late at night.

He felt refreshed, though surprised he had slept for so long and so deeply.

He wasn't sure just what it was that had disturbed him; something at odds with the normal nightsounds of the town, he guessed. But — what? Then he tensed at a small noise coming from above his dark bunk.

It was metal scraping across stone. *That* was the sound that had awakened him.

He stood up, frowning at the high barred window, too high for him to see out of even if he stood on the bunk. Then he saw it moving down the wall — a shadow sliding down towards the bunk.

At first he thought it was one of the giant tarantulas that sometimes found their way up here, all the way from the

Gulf country. Then as his eyes grew more accustomed to the dim light he realized it was his way out.

His one and only chance to escape the gallows!

A gun was being lowered into his cell on a string.

He crouched on the blankets, reached up swiftly and tugged. The string came sliding through the bars, unimpeded, and he held a sixgun between his hands. No use trying to see who had sent him this means of escape but he called hoarsely, 'Thanks, *amigo*!'

Then he snapped the string where it was tied around the trigger-guard, checked that the cylinder was loaded and paused to think out his next move . . .

★   ★   ★

He stepped to the barred door and called hoarsely to the night deputy who was likely dozing in the front office.

129

'Deputy! *Deputy!* I need ... help ...'

He dropped to one knee, forehead resting on the cool iron bars, the sixgun hidden down by his thigh away from the side on which the guard would approach. His stomach growled emptily and he tried to ignore the gnawing hunger. He hung there, one arm hanging limply through the bars, resting on a cross-piece.

'*Deputy!*' He began to cough and hawk noisily.

The man came warily, hand on gun-butt, watching that limply dangling arm. He was a barrel-bellied man with a bald head; what hair he had hung almost to his shoulders, he had a greasy fringe.

'The hell's the matter with you, Wade? No, I ain't comin' any closer yet — I've had you in the cells before, with some of your hell-raisers, but they ain't here to help you this time. Left days ago. So you got any notion of ...'

Wade allowed himself to slide down

on to both knees, the legs going from under him so that he sat on the stone floor, his right hand still hidden. He made his eyes bulge and worked his moist lips, trying to speak, spittle flying.

'Roach!' he choked, clawing at his throat. 'On my grub. Didn't see it — caught — caught in my throat . . . '

The big deputy grimaced at the picture of one of the big Laredo cockroaches jammed in a man's throat, hawked noisily and spat. But still he hesitated. Wade began to make strangled sounds, clawing at his throat, rolling his upper body wildly, coughing hackingly, trying to retch . . .

The deputy swore, fumbled up his keys and unlocked the door. He swung it open but stepped back.

'Crawl out here an' lemme see your hands — *both* of 'em!'

Coughing still, gasping and making awful wheezing sounds, his face congested, Matthew Wade started to crawl out of the cell. The deputy crouched, waiting, hand on gun-butt.

'Both hands I said!'

Wade had tied the string through a handle of the tray holding his cold supper, still balanced on the bar of the slot. He yanked and the whole kit and caboodle clattered to the floor with one hell of a crashing commotion.

The deputy leapt a foot in the air, heart hammering as he swung towards the unexpected sound, palming up his gun — or trying to. He fumbled in his shock and next second his wrist was jarred and throbbing as his gun thudded to the passage floor. Wade's rising body cannoned into him and slammed him back against the wall, the muzzle of his Colt pressing up under the man's unshaven jaw.

'Get down on your hands and knees and just using your fingertips, move into that cell . . . Because I'm moving out!'

8

'Way Down South'

The deputy's arms were tied tightly with the string from wrists to elbows, behind his back, and he was gagged with his own neckerchief. He lay on the cell bunk, struggling vainly and cursing a blue streak behind the gag.

In the front office, Matthew Wade hurriedly collected his sixgun rig, the weapon that had been passed to him in his cell resting on a corner of the sheriff's desk. He had his back to the door as he buckled the cartridge belt around his waist and froze as the door opened and a voice said:

'Renny, when Roy comes in in the mornin', tell him that . . . *Judas!*'

Wade spun, the belt still only half-buckled, the holster hanging awkwardly so that he fumbled as he grabbed for his Colt. It was too late. Steve Kendrick stood just inside the street-door, holding a cocked pistol, a crooked smile beginning on his battered face.

'Well damned if I know how you did it, Matt, but this is as far as you go!' The gun-barrel jerked an inch. 'Lift 'em!'

Wade's mouth tightened as he obeyed, the cartridge-belt dragging at his upper legs.

'I was hoping to run into you before I left, Steve.'

Kendrick laughed. 'Sure you were! But not this way!'

Wade said nothing and then there was a small movement behind Kendrick and suddenly the man's back arched as he was shoved violently forward into the office, staggering. In a second, Wade scooped up the gun from the edge of the desk and hurled it into Kendrick's midriff. The man gagged, stumbled, half doubled over. Wade kicked free of the impeding gunbelt, brought up his knee into Kendrick's face, sending the man crashing against the wall. He scooped up the sixgun from the floor and smashed it across Steve's head.

The troubleshooter grunted and collapsed in an untidy heap, huddled against the wall, a little blood oozing from his nostrils. Only then did Wade look towards the door, which had been closed.

Leaning against it, wide-eyed, was Merida.

His jaw sagged a little and then he frowned.

'What're you doing here?'

It came out rougher than he had meant it to, but his surprise at seeing her had hit him like a fist in the teeth.

He saw her face tighten.

'I come to help!'

He looked down at the pistol in his hand.

'You?'

She nodded, her eyes glistening.

'Well, I guess we can figure out the

135

why and how later. We better get out of here.'

She nodded, her raven-dark hair shimmering in the dim glow of the lamp.

'Better we use the back door.' She turned and dropped the locking bar across the brackets on the street-door.

A couple of minutes later they were amongst the weeds in the small yard behind the jail. She groped for his hand and held it tightly as they made their way to a side fence and a gate. She started away towards a line of dark trees, but he held back.

'I have to get my rifle and warbag.'

'Is dangerous!'

'Not as dangerous as going on the run without 'em. It won't take long.'

He knew Laredo well enough, better than the girl, and led the way through back streets and weedgrown lanes. There were still a few folk on Main but then there were always a few folk on the streets of Laredo every hour of the day and night. If they couldn't find enough fun in Laredo itself, the revellers simply crossed over to Nuevo Laredo on the Mexican side and when they had had enough, made their way back north across the Rio.

No one tried to stop them.

Wade was counting on that for when he cleared town. But the girl . . .

As they made their way carefully along a creek bank in the direction of Mrs O'Shane's, he asked:

'How come you're here, Merida? But first — I'm obliged for what you did.'

She shrugged. 'You save my life, Mateo. I am here with Roca.'

That stopped him in his tracks and he grabbed her arm, pulling her off balance. She fell against him, hands going around him, but she made no move to step back even when she had her balance.

'Rocky brought you here?'

'*Sí*. He tell me how you only let Don Diego take me because you think it safer for me.' Her voice softened. 'Oh,

137

you do care — a little — for me, Mateo?'

'Sure I do,' he said shortly, wondering just when he had told Rocky he thought the girl would be safer with Diego than travelling north with him.

The girl went on to tell him briefly that Rocky had left Don Diego and had brought her with him to Laredo. 'To be with you, Mateo!' she added a little breathlessly.

They weren't moving now; Wade was trying to savvy this. He knew Rocky of old, the man wouldn't do such a thing without reason . . . and a damn good one at that.

He had thought the girl was nervous, but had put it down to the present situation, and her expectations at being with him again. But maybe there was something more underlying it.

'Don Diego wouldn't take kindly to you going with Rocky — or even him quitting. What made him do it?'

She didn't seem to want to answer, but at his probing told him that Rocky had asked her to get Diego's part of the treasure-map; Rocky knew where it was kept in the *ranchero*'s bedroom and Merida was in the best position to get her hands on it.

'When Don Diego sleep,' she said quietly, giving him an up-from-under look. He nodded briefly, letting her know he understood what she was implying. 'I get the map and take it to Rocky, but he must look at it first — and it go bad.'

'What d'you mean? Go bad?'

'Noah come.'

'Christ!'

'Rocky hit him with water-canteen he have but Noah shoot him.' She touched her head above her left ear. 'Here.'

'Rocky's dead?'

'No, no, but hurt. We run. He had already arranged a trail leading south to the sierra country. When we get here we hear you are in jail.'

'And you helped me break out! This is a helluva thing, Merida! Not sure I savvy it properly, but it'll do for now.

We've got to clear town before Diego comes.'

'He look in the Sierra.'

Wade stopped and looked back. 'Not for long. Not with that Noah. He'll soon figure it's a false trail. Come on! You don't realize just how dangerous this is, Merida.'

She caught up with him, and her teeth flashed in the night.

'I with you now, Mateo.'

'Yeah!' he said heavily, cursing Rocky under his breath.

As they hurried towards the rooming-house, she told him that Rocky was waiting in abandoned adobe ruins west of the town, near a trickle of a creek and some willows. Wade knew the place and by the time he had collected his gear in his room, he knew what he was going to do.

'Merida, in the back of that closet you'll find my jacket. Likely on the floor . . . '

'Sí, Mateo.' She opened the door and went inside the small closet, peering into the shadows.

In seconds, he had the door closed and locked and she was hammering on the inside, calling his name, then cursing him.

'Best this way, Merida. Mrs O'Shane'll take care of you. When Diego learns Rocky and me quit town, he'll figure you went with us.'

He couldn't make out the words but he knew she wasn't praising him.

'I'll get back when I can or make some arrangements for you.'

Her small fists hammered on the door panel.

'You sonna beech!'

He heard that all right and smiled faintly. '*Hasta la vista*, Merida.'

Mrs O'Shane met him in the passage and her face was not friendly. He apologized for the noise, took her arm and hurried her downstairs into the kitchen. The Irish woman protested all the way, yet was puzzled by this normally polite man's rough behaviour.

He briefly explained that Merida was

the daughter of an old friend and she'd run away from a Mexican *ranchero* who had kept her as his mistress. Mrs O'Shane was outraged and immediately compassionate.

'Ah, the poor dear, so she is! And she came to you for protection. But wait! By the saints, you're supposed to be in jail, Matthew Wade!'

He glossed over how he had escaped and took money from his warbag.

'This is for taking care of Merida. They'll come looking but they want me and a pard worse than they want her. If you can hide her until it's safe . . . ?'

'Just let this damn arrogant greaser try to get his hands on her and I'll chop them off with my meat-cleaver, so I will!'

That was good enough for Wade. Twenty minutes later he was confronting Rocky Calloway in the adobe ruins. The man met him with a gun in his hand, a crude bandage about his head.

Rocky let out a long breath as he eased down the gun-hammer.

'Hell, good to see you, Matt! Where's the gal?'

'I hid her with a friend.'

Rocky arched his eyebrows, then smiled.

'Hey, good idea! I had to use you as bait to get her to do a little job for me . . .'

'Steal Diego's map, you mean. Yeah, she told me.'

Rocky was a mite wary now.

'Well, she was in the best position to get her hands on it . . .'

'But you'd seen it before. Why did you want her to steal it?'

'Long story, Matt. We better get goin'. I've got hosses out the back.'

'Checked 'em on the way in. Rocky, I don't take to you lying to that girl, letting her believe I want her with me.'

Rocky laughed and winced, clapping a hand to his head-wound.

'Well, she's a looker. Don't tell me you've changed *that* much!'

'She's a kid. Impressionable. I can't have her tailing me around everywhere.

And you damn well know that.'

Rocky shrugged. 'I needed a look at that map.'

'You can be a real son of a bitch at times, Rocky. I still don't savvy why you needed to see it when . . . ' He stopped suddenly. 'Hell! You said Diego had you searching for the second part of that map. You found it, didn't you?'

Rocky smiled crookedly.

'And it's gonna make us rich, *amigo*! I can remember some of Diego's part and matched up with mine. It puts us right in the Sierra in the Llano Blanco area! Right where you spent all that time lookin' for Geronimo!'

Wade stared at him.

'You owe me, Matt! I got you outta jail, saved your neck.'

'You got me out? I thought it was Merida.'

'Whose shoulders you think she stood on so she could lower that sixgun into your cell?'

Wade released a long breath.

'Well, we've got to get outta here anyway, and, with a murder charge hanging over my head, I need to go south.'

Rocky grinned, punched him lightly on the shoulder. 'That's what I want to hear! Let's go.' They made for the tethered horses and Wade thought: he doesn't care about the girl. He's used her and now she's no longer his concern.

Yeah. Rocky Calloway had sure changed over the years. And not for the better . . .

*　*　*

'They'll make for the Rio! Goddamnit, Steve, how the hell did you let him get away?'

Steve Kendrick glared at Sheriff Roy Engels as he held a cold-water-soaked cloth to the knot on his head. It was bleeding a little, his vision was queer and he was in no mood for the lawman's bitching.

'Was your man Renny let him get outta the cell.'

Engels grunted. 'Yeah, well he'd gotten a gun from somewhere. All right, we better check the bridge and if he ain't been spotted we'll have to ride the river. Ain't no way he's still hangin' around town. He'll *have* to get across the border and whoever helped him is likely with him . . . '

'You go get him. I'm too poorly.' Kendrick scowled and the look he gave the sheriff made Roy Engels pause as he was about to berate the man.

'OK. Renny can get on down to the bridge and if he can't find anythin' I'll roust out Finn and we'll ride the river. And you'd better ride with us, Steve. I'm holdin' you partly responsible for this.'

'Go to hell.'

The sheriff swore, grabbed rifle and sixgun, bawled for Renny, the disgraced deputy, and sent the man down to the bridge across into Nuevo Laredo. He went out to a lean-to built on to the

146

side of the building and rousted out Deputy Finn, telling the sleepy man to saddle some horses, that they had a jailbreak on their hands.

By that time Renny had returned to the office with negative news: Matthew Wade had not been spotted crossing into Mexico, but a cowboy, sleeping off some booze out of town near the old adobe ruins, had happened to see some lights inside there, and what he thought were two men moving about.

'That'll be them!' Engels said without any further proof. He and the two deputies left hurriedly while Steve Kendrick wet his bloodstained cloth again, wrung it out over the tin basin and held it to his head-wound. He dozed in the chair . . .

* * *

Rocky Calloway wasn't as spry as he thought. When he stood up quickly after Wade came back with the saddled horses, he swayed and had to grab at the broken adobe wall for support.

'You OK?' Wade asked.

'Kind of dizzy. Got me one helluva headache and I ain't seein' so good.'

Wade helped him aboard a big grey, settled him in leather then kicked dirt over the small fire and mounted his black mare. Calloway swayed a little, grabbing at the saddle horn and Wade took the grey's reins, leading it away from the adobe ruins towards the distant river.

'We can't use the bridge. They'd remember you half falling out of the saddle. We'll have to swim the horses across.'

'OK, OK! I'll be all right!' Rocky sounded agitated, annoyed with himself for showing what he figured was a weakness. 'I been OK up till now, and I'll be from here on in, so let's go!'

Wade stared briefly, remembering Rocky's stubbornness from the past, his dislike for anything that made him even temporarily dependent on anyone else.

The river was wider than he remembered and, although it narrowed downstream, he didn't want to go back towards town where lights would be reflected in the dark water and maybe show them up while they made their crossing. Rocky was fighting to stay upright, cursing every so often, wishing he had a bottle of whiskey.

Wade still held the grey's reins, called softly to 'hold on' while he worked the animals down the bank. The water was cool against his legs and the horse snorted as it rose above his belly. Rocky's grey pulled back a little and Calloway, not ready for it, spilled into the shallows. He was mighty angry, lashed out at the horse, punching it on the ear and falling backwards again with a large splash.

The grey plunged away with a snorting whinny.

'Real smart move, Rock!' gritted Wade, spurring after the animal.

It led him a short chase along the river, the steepness of the bank keeping them in the shallows, spray flying, and hoofs churning the water to a muddy colour — and not silently. Wade was swearing to himself by the time he leaned from the saddle and snatched the grey's trailing reins, hauling the animal to a halt. It still fought, but its heart wasn't in it now, and he led it back to where Rocky waited, fists clenched.

'Just get into leather and leave the hoss be,' Wade told him. 'Getting into Mexico's more important than . . . '

'Hey! You two men!' A voice bellowed out of the night abruptly. 'Stay where you are! We're comin' down!'

'Engels!' hissed Wade, tossing Rocky the grey's reins. 'You manage?'

'Damn right!' Calloway snapped, coming fully alert now. He slid his sixgun from his cross-draw holster even as he touched the skittish grey's flanks with his spurs.

The grey snickered and leapt forward into the river with a splash. Immediately, two rifles crashed and Wade heard the zip of lead tearing into the muddy water. He spurred the black forward, palming up his own sixgun, shooting at the gun-flashes, ducking low along the black's back. The guns answered and men shouted as they plunged their horses down into the river. One man's mount slipped in the mud and threw him. He surged up out of the water, roaring, soaked, shooting wildly.

The gunfire tore the peaceful night apart and Wade knew it must he heard in Laredo. He triggered at a dark shape plunging out towards him, saw the horse rear up, pawing water and air, going over sideways with a mighty splash, throwing its rider. Rocky was shooting fast and wild, using his rifle now.

The lawmen urged their mounts out into the river, trying to stop the fugitives from reaching the Mexican shore.

Engels was yelling, the only one mounted now. His two deputies were in the river, Renny in the shallows, shooting, but Finn gulping water and struggling to get back to where he could put his feet on the bottom, deathly afraid, for like most Westerners, he was a poor swimmer.

'Don't let 'em reach the other bank, goddamnit!' bawled Roy Engels, voice cracking with his intensity. He kept his horse plunging forward, shot until his rifle was empty then, panting, slid out of the saddle into the water alongside his swimming mount, slowly turning it back towards the Texas side. *He couldn't touch Wade on Mexican soil . . .*

Ahead, he saw the dim shapes of Wade and Calloway heaving their mounts up into Mexico, not pausing at the top of the slope, but riding hell for leather away into the dark night and deep into Mañana Land.

'Son of a *bitch*!' Engels snapped, then urged his mount back towards Texas and his half-drowned deputies.

9

Hunter and Hunted

Steve Kendrick looked hard at Roy Engels in the sheriff's office the next morning. It was not long past daylight and the lawman was red-eyed and in a bad mood. Certainly no mood for Kendrick's criticisms.

'Damnit, Roy! What in hell's the matter with you? You had the sonuver cold! All you had to do was shoot across the goddamn river as he climbed out the other side and we wouldn't have no more worries!'

Engels locked his fingers, the knuckles white. He tried to speak calmly, though he forced his words through his yellowed teeth.

'That's what you reckon, huh? Well, you weren't there, Steve! If you had've been, mebbe Wade and his sidekick would be dead right now! But, no, you had to stay and nurse a bit of a headache!' His voice rose and shouted down the freight-man as Kendrick tried to defend his excuses.

'I had one man half-drownin' and in a panic, the other up to his balls in mud tryin' to climb out of the river, and I was *out of ammunition*! Now, you tell me how I was gonna nail Wade — in the dark, too! It's new moon, in case you hadn't noticed, no light worth a damn!'

Kendrick sighed and settled into the visitors' chair across the desk from the sheriff. He nodded jerkily.

'Yeah, OK, OK! You see who his pard was?'

Engels shook his head, still glaring, still angry.

'Well, he got away. And now he knows we been runnin' guns across the Rio. Judas, Roy, we could be in a helluva lot of trouble!'

'We *are* in a helluva lot of trouble. But I don't see Wade comin' back soon and it ain't likely he'll bother tellin' anyone down in Mañana Land about us. Still, I'd be a lot happier if he was dead.' He squinted at Kendrick. 'You wouldn't want to take a little trip south and see to it, huh?'

Kendrick's turn to scowl.

'Not me. I got other fish to fry up here and Brennan'll be screamin' soon if I don't head back to San Antonio.'

'Well, *I* can't touch him. We'll just have to wait and see what happens . . . '

They didn't have long to wait.

Mid-morning, Don Diego Corzo arrived with Noah and half a dozen carefully chosen *pistoleros*, all heavily armed and eager to earn the promised bounty for tracking down Rocky Calloway and Merida.

The *ranchero* made himself known to Engels, who knew him by sight but had had nothing to do with him in person until now.

'I look for a man named Calloway, Rocky Calloway,' the Don explained in the sheriff's small office. Noah leaned against one wall, silently, his face immobile as usual, thumbs hooked in the crossed cartridge-belts he wore with his long-barrelled Smith & Wesson pistols in their cutaway holsters. Just his presence made Engels uneasy.

Kendrick also had been in the office when Diego arrived, on his way back to San Antonio. He too was now included in the discussion as Diego outlined his problem.

Engels let the *ranchero* finish, then sighed.

'Don Diego, I'm sorry to tell you that I had Matthew Wade locked up in my cells until last night. Someone busted him out and I reckon it would've been this Calloway. They jumped the Rio into Mexico. Out of my jurisdiction.'

Noah had straightened up but his expression didn't change. Diego glanced at him, then set his dark gaze on the sheriff.

'The girl was with them?'

Engels shook his head. 'No gal. Just two men, one wearin' what might've been a bandage around his head. His hat was hanging down his back by the chin-strap, was how I seen it.'

'Roca!' hissed the Don. '*Sí*, Señor Calloway was slightly wounded in the head by Noah. But he fled with the girl. They tried to confuse us with a trail leading south but we soon realized it was a trick. She has . . . an attraction . . . to this Wade. She would come to Laredo with Calloway.'

He stressed these last words, hard eyes flicking from the sheriff to Kendrick, silently accusing.

Engels shook his head.

'Know nothin' about any gal.'

'And you, *señor*?' Diego asked a thoughtful Kendrick.

Steve shook his head.

'Never seen her but — well, Wade's a queer *hombre*, Don Diego. Got this . . . code he lives by. I dunno if he's taken a shine to this *señorita* or not . . . '

'I think — no,' the Don said quietly. 'Perhaps he has some . . . feeling for her. She wanted to go with him to

157

Laredo another time, but he . . . left her with me. For safety, according to Calloway.'

Kendrick snapped his fingers.

'That's the kinda thing he would do — and what I was thinkin' of.' He flicked his gaze to the Mexican's face. 'You — er — offering a reward or anything?'

Diego Corzo's face reflected his distaste but he nodded readily enough.

'There could be some *pesos* involved. But I am not prepared to name a sum at this time. You think you have some information?'

'Not — exactly information, but sort of an informed guess.' He held up a hand as Noah turned towards him, eyes narrowing. 'Listen a moment. Wade's a sucker for lame ducks. If he thought the gal was in danger, he wouldn't take her with him back to Mexico. He'd stash her somewhere she'd be safe.'

Diego leaned forward.

'And that would be . . . where?'

Kendrick smiled.

'He uses the same roomin'-house every time he's in Laredo. There's a tough old Irish woman runs it, but she's all mush underneath. It's just possible he asked her to look after the gal.'

Diego was on his feet and Noah was already taking Kendrick's arm, pulling him upright out of his chair before the man even finished speaking.

* * *

It took very little time for Mrs O'Shane to control her first burst of anger and tell Don Diego what he wanted to know. Noah put away his matches and set down the uncapped bottle of coal-oil as the *pistolero* who had been holding the Irish woman released her. She slumped in a chair, biting her lower lip as she massaged her all-but-dislocated shoulder.

'A pox on yer!' she hissed. Moments later two Mexicans dragged the struggling Merida into the big kitchen.

'I'm sorry, darlin',' Mrs O'Shane

gasped. 'They were goin' to burn down me house, so they were!'

Merida didn't look at her. Her big round brown eyes were on Diego's face and she was pale, her slim young body trembling. The *ranchero* stepped forward, pushed some strands of her glistening raven hair away from her face. He touched her smooth cheek lightly with his fingers and she flinched.

'Such beauty. So smooth, so . . . unblemished.'

Merida began speaking rapidly in Spanish, struggling to get free of the men holding her as their fingers dug deep into her young flesh. There were tears and her knees were weak. She was pleading in her efforts to explain.

'I just wanted to come and be with Mateo!' she finished lamely, in English.

Diego pursed his lips and nodded, seeming to understand.

'Of course. But I treated you well, Merida. I gave you much better things than Mateo Wade could ever offer you . . . '

'But for how long?' she burst out and then looked sorry she had spoken.

Diego shrugged. '*Sí*, it would not have been for ever. But no matter now. You will tell me where Roca and Wade have gone and perhaps you will remain as beautiful as you are at this moment.'

Her eyes seemed to widen ever more. 'But I don't know! Mateo lock me in closet! Then he go with Roca.'

Diego lost patience and slapped her. Hard. Her hair flew wildly about her face and shoulders. The men holding her almost lost their grip as she jerked with the impact. Her legs sagged and they pulled her upright. The imprint of Diego's hand was a white stencil on her left cheek. Mrs O'Shane started to speak, but when Noah placed a hand on her injured shoulder she stopped abruptly.

Diego took the sobbing girl's jaw between his finger and thumb and forced her head up, looking deeply into her tear-filled eyes. There was a bead of blood at the corner of her mouth. He spoke calmly.

'You stole my portion of the map. You were studying it with Roca and his portion when Noah found you both. You dropped my map, but Roca took his part with him. You must have seen enough to know which part of the Sierra Roca's map showed.'

Merida was silent for a short time and he allowed her breathing to return to more or less normal. Then she nodded.

'Is somewhere in the Llano Blanco, not far from the *pantano* — *la cienaga*.'

'The swamp!' Diego said hoarsely. 'Of course! They speak of a *lago* in the papers my family have! A lake could become a swamp easily in several hundred years!'

'Perhaps the treasure was thrown into the swamp,' Merida suggested, a touch of viciousness in her tone.

Diego smiled coldly. 'Then you will swim and retrieve it for me, *querida*.'

'I?' The girl looked horrified.

'Perhaps,' he said casually. 'You told me once you were reared in the Sierra Madre. I think you will come with me.'

'Oh, no, Don Diego! No! Not back into the Sierra!'

Diego merely jerked his head at Noah. The man signed to the two men holding Merida and they dragged her out.

Roy Engels had been silent up until now, but spoke up suddenly, startling Kendrick.

'Steve here knows the Sierra Madre pretty good, Don Diego. He's a handy man with a gun, too. Could be to your advantage to have him along.'

'Now wait up!' started Kendrick, but Engels flashed a warning look at him. Kendrick knew what the sheriff was thinking: if he went with Diego he could make sure Wade's mouth was shut pronto before he had a chance to say anything about Kendrick's and the sheriff's implication in gun-running. Diego would kill them both if he knew.

'I'm expected back in San Antonio,'

Steve said lamely.

Diego smiled thinly. 'I can appease Marc Brennan for you, Señor Kendrick. I think it could be to the advantage of us both if you accompanied us. It is settled.'

Kendrick swore softly at Engels, moving his lips carefully so that the smirking sheriff could read them easily.

* * *

'He's still there!'

Rocky Calloway stirred himself in the shade of the large boulder and stood, shading his eyes as he stared at the dusty, worn boots belonging to Matthew Wade. Wade was stretched out on his belly atop the rock, propped on his elbows as he looked through the battered brass-and-leather field-glasses.

Rocky climbed up with a couple of easy swings, keeping low as he clambered up alongside his partner, and held out his left hand. Wade gave him the glasses; Calloway adjusted focus and searched the rugged canyon country they had passed through last night.

He saw the horse first; a dirty-white colour with a sprinkle of dark-brown shapes over the rump, which gave the animal a dingy, unkempt aspect. But he knew no matter how it looked, that horse was powerful, had the stamina of a cougar in search of a mate, and could run faster than that particular member of the big cat family.

Nearby, a man crouched on one knee, examining the ground with deliberation, picking up a stone, turning it carefully in his hand, looking at it on all sides. When the inspection was completed, he put it back into the exact place he had taken it from and picked up another.

Calloway swore softly.

'That goddamn Noah! He ain't a man. He's half wolf and half devil.'

'We've got to stop him, Rocky,' Wade said, rolling on to his side. His face was gaunt and stubbled with beard that glowed like gold wire when the hot sunlight blazed through it. 'This is four days he's been way out in front of Don Diego's posse, and he's led 'em right along our trail. Damned if I know what to do to cover our tracks any more. I'd swear we left no more sign than a puff of smoke but that damn Mex is back there only a mile or two behind.'

Calloway shook his head.

'Nothin' to be done, *amigo*. He's the best there is — and I mean the best! He can track a legless fly in a brushfire. Ain't no way to stop him.'

'We'll have to kill him.'

Calloway snatched the glasses from Wade's eyes and turned to look at him.

'Thought you weren't a killer no more?'

'Where'd you get that idea? I figure it's necessary . . . ' He paused and shrugged. Then he frowned at the way Calloway smiled crookedly. 'What's wrong?'

'Just had a picture of you and Noah havin' at it. You with no practice for years, an' him whippin' out them old

S&Ws and shootin' you full of holes.'
He laughed and shook his head again.
'Man! You wouldn't stand a chance!'

'I was thinking of bushwhacking
him,' Wade said shortly, irritated by
Calloway's attitude.

Calloway arched his eyebrows. 'So!
You have still got that killer-instinct
buried inside you!'

'I do what's necessary — and if we
don't stop that Mex, we're gonna wake
up one morning with Don Diego and
his riders sitting in our camp waiting
for breakfast.'

Calloway sobered and both men
moved back a little on the boulder as
Noah mounted his horse, looked in
their general direction, then moved his
head slowly in a half-circle as if making
up his mind which way to move.

In moments, he was taking the trail
out of the canyon that would lead him
unerringly into the Sierra foothills,
where they waited.

'Damn! He's got mighty good
instincts!'

'You bet. And forget ambush. He'll be expecting it and he'll be ready. We'll never nail him. I tell you, Matt, I've been around Mexes and Injuns and outlaws for a good many years, but I've never seen anyone like this Noah. Must be in his fifties but he's tough as a *brasada* mustang and as ruthless as a rattler when you step on it.'

Wade lowered the glasses, his mouth tight.

'He's figured we'd make for high ground because of that ridge between us and the pass. But how would he know what part of the Sierra we're making for? You said Diego's part of the map didn't show that, only your section.'

'Must've been the gal. She seemed to know the Llano Blanco pretty well. Born near there, I think.'

Wade frowned. 'She wouldn't tell Diego, would she?'

Calloway smiled faintly. 'Mebbe she wouldn't *want* to tell him, but she'd tell anyway in the end.'

'Providing he found her at Ma O'Shane's.'

'If he was lookin' he'd have found her . . .'

They slid down from the boulder, rolled cigarettes and fired them up in the shade.

'I'm gonna try an ambush,' Wade decided. 'I'll shoot his bronc out from under him.'

'Better not. Get Noah first, let the hoss go. But he's uncanny, Matt. He'll be expectin' us to try — which is why he hasn't bothered to hide himself when he's trackin'. You'll never get close enough for a good bead.'

'We've got to do something! He'll lead Diego and his posse right to us, otherwise.'

'Well, you can try if you want. Me, I'm headin' on. I'll wait for you at Los Alamitos. But only till sundown. If you ain't there by then, I'll know you ain't comin'.'

'Thanks for the vote of confidence!'

Rocky put a hand on Wade's arm as

the man placed a foot in the stirrup of his horse.

'Matt, we can try to outrun 'em. We ride all night we can . . . '

'We'll miss landmarks and I need to find 'em if we're gonna search the Blanco area. I'll try my way, Rock. And I will see you at Los Alamitos.'

Calloway sighed.

'Well, I'll be lookin' for you, pard.'

But he didn't sound too sure.

★　★　★

Wade drew bead on the head of the dirty-white horse as it stopped in between some rocks either side of the unmarked trail. There was a bush in the way that could deflect a bullet at this range, but Noah had deliberately chosen this place to halt so as not to reveal himself.

The man was unbelievable: he must sense something for he didn't simply pause and then nudge the mount forward, inch by inch. He didn't move.

170

Wade made his decision.

A man afoot in this country, even a man like Noah, was at a mighty big disadvantage.

He fired without any further thought and saw the horse jerk its head, rear up and go down thrashing. He put two bullets through the bush at vague movements behind it and saw a blur of something moving fast through the branches.

He half rose and tracked the movement, levering and triggering two more shots as fast as an eye-blink. There was a dull crash of branches snapping and a cloud of dust rose behind the bush. Wade shot through it, knowing Noah had deliberately kicked it up so as to screen his movements.

The man was good, all right.

Wade traversed with each remaining shot in the magazine, hastily thumbed home fresh loads into the under-barrel tube. The dust cleared slowly but there were no more movements. The horse had stopped thrashing now.

There was no return fire.

He began to sweat — he had been sweating for days in this hammering heat in the baked country of the Sierra, but this time the sweat was tinged with chill.

The man below — if he was still there — was like no other he had tackled over the years. A man with discipline enough not to shoot back immediately after ambush was someone to reckon with. And if Noah moved ghostlike as Calloway claimed, he could be even now stalking Wade, ready for the kill.

But Wade had instincts, too, and none of them told him that this was the case. He didn't feel as if he was being stalked by a killer. But Noah wouldn't run. Hell, where was there to run to, anyway? Beyond the point where the horse had been shot there was only the steep, rock-studded, broken slope that Wade could see from his elevated position amongst the boulders. If Noah didn't run down that slope he had to stay put or crab across right or left on rock that would crumble with the first pressure put on it. So he had to . . .

Wade stood up, unable to stop himself.

Noah wasn't running, he was dropping down that deadly exposed slope, plunging so that his boots barely touched the ground, arms flailing for balance, hardly raising any dust, the fall was so steep where he was.

Steep enough for the rim to screen him from Wade even as the freighter managed to get off one shot that ricocheted from the edge, chewing rock splinters and grit. The man had taken his chance — exposed himself for the first few seconds of the fall, gambling that the shock of such a manoeuvre would freeze any action on Wade's part momentarily, just long enough for him to drop out of sight below the rim where he would be safe.

Matthew Wade thumbed back his hat; Calloway was right. He'd never come up against anyone like this deadly

Mexican before ... And he seemed unstoppable!

He waited because there was nothing else to do, trying to get inside Noah's head, figure where he would have to come out. But, of course, Noah didn't.

Wade had reckoned on the right place all right, but Noah didn't expose himself. Instead, a column of thick white-brown smoke rose up out of the canyon as Noah threw green brush on to the fire he had made.

It would make a fine target for Don Diego's posse to home in on.

10

Pistols in the Dark

The Place of the Little Shaking Poplars — Los Alamitos — was a good place to make a camp. And Rocky Calloway had decided to make it a cold camp so that Matthew Wade had some trouble locating him.

When he did he told Calloway about Noah and the fire as he chewed on some jerky, washed it down with a mouthful of water. Rocky swore.

'Told you he was tricky.' He started gathering up their gear at once. 'We'll have to move on. It'll be dark pretty soon.'

Wade hesitated. 'I've been trying to figure what Noah'll do next. He knows we won't stick around, that we'll realize that column of smoke will bring in Diego's posse. But you can bet he'll be out in front again.'

'Hell, yeah! C'mon — let's get movin'. We can talk in the saddle.'

Still Wade made no move.

'I'll wait for him here.'

Calloway paused with one boot in the stirrup.

'You'll — what?'

Wade kept chewing without speaking. Rocky dropped his foot to the ground and stood there, holding the saddle horn, looking strangely at Wade.

'You're loco,' he said quietly.

'Mebbe. Mebbe not. Noah might expect ambush, but I reckon he won't be expecting a square-off.'

'Judas, man, you're crazy! You have to be. For a start, I doubt you'll get the jump on Noah, and if you do, he's like a bolt of lightnin' with them *pistolas*. I've seen him in action. No warnin', no moves that tell you he's ready to go, just — gunsmoke. And he walks away. *Every — damn — time*!'

'Except this time.'

Calloway frowned. 'How come you're

so confident of a sudden? You told me you ain't bothered practisin' your draw. It's been years! You can't just rely on the old talent with that long a lay-off.'

'All right, Rocky. You stay, too, and we'll get him in a crossfire.'

Rocky laughed without humour. 'That'll be the day!'

'We don't stop him, we're never going to make the Blanco country. Even if we do, Diego's gonna be snapping at our heels. So — Noah has to be stopped.'

Calloway hesitated, then swung up into the saddle.

'I know too much about him to try what you want. You got any sense, you'll ride with me right now. I hope you make it, Matt, but . . . ' He shrugged, flicked a brief salute from the brim of his hat and spurred away.

'So that's that,' Wade murmured as he watched Calloway swallowed up by the trees.

He finished eating, took a mouthful more of water, then slung the canteen from the saddle again. Los Alamitos was already in deep shadow amongst the trees but there was still a golden afterglow beyond.

Wade made his preparations without hurry. He hitched the horse, leaving it saddled to a bush well away from the small clearing he had chosen as his meeting-place with Noah. Then he sat down against a tree, took out his sixgun and cleaned and oiled it without taking it to pieces. The action was much smoother when he had finished and the rifling in the barrel gleamed with the last of the afterglow when he held it up to his eye. The hammer was smooth and cocked with a silky, satisfying *click*. He removed six fresh cartridges from his belt loops, rubbed the brass cases and bullets on the oily rag, removing any trace of oxide build-up and dust that had collected. They slid home smoothly into their chambers and the cylinder spun slickly.

Lastly, he rubbed neatsfoot oil into the leather on the inside of the holster, smeared a little on the bulges of the gun frame: the loading gate, the cylinder fluting, the ramrod beneath the barrel, any part that could conceivably snag even for a fraction of a second.

He had no illusions about facing Noah; even allowing for some exaggeration on Rocky's part, the man was the most dangerous Wade had ever faced.

He waited.

He wasn't going in figuring not to lose — he was going in figuring to *win*. It was the only way:there was no second place in such a contest, only one winner and one loser. You're either fast or last, and last is for ever.

Darkness closed in as if someone had dropped a huge blanket over the clump of trees. Night sounds surrounded him. The leaves rustled in a light breeze that bore with it the desiccated smell of the kiln-dry Sierra only a few miles beyond.

Water would be the biggest problem out there. Water and dust. No amount of precautions would be able to hide the dust raised in those snarled, mummified ridges. Diego wouldn't need a guide then — just a good observer.

But Noah still had to be stopped. There was something about the man that put a chill in Wade's very blood and . . .

His heart smashed against his ribs as a shadow abruptly stepped into the clearing opposite where he waited.

Good Christ! He hadn't heard a thing!

Surely Noah must hear the way his heart was banging! He moved an arm and his shirt rubbed briefly against his bent knee. Cotton against denim.

Noah stopped in his small movement of looking around. Wade's breath trickled silently between his teeth; he must have a lot of Indian in him, he figured, to have hearing like that.

He froze, feeling the man's stare moving towards his position — then stopping. Hell! Noah must have cat-eyes as well to pick him out in this light against the dark background he had chosen.

'You are the one who killed my horse.'

Wade was shocked. It was a woman's voice! It came out of Noah, all right, but in the dark it could well be mistaken for a woman's.

'And now I'm going to kill you,' Wade said, rising lithely, smoothly and carefully.

'Many have tried.'

'I will succeed.'

'I will carve those words on your headstone. I have carved many headstones.'

'You won't carve mine.'

Noah shrugged. 'Shall we see?'

The words surprised Wade a little although they shouldn't have: there was no shade of fear in this man. He was supremely confident in the knowledge he had never lost a gunfight.

Nor had Wade. But the last one had been almost ten years ago . . .

'Might as well get it done,' he said,

mouth dry. 'You want to call?'

Again Noah shrugged. 'Whenever you wish to make your move I am ready.'

'Then — *now!*'

The grove of trees shook to the blast of gunfire, two shots sounding as one, the concussion disturbing dead leaves on the ground, the spurts of gunsmoke shrouding both men momentarily.

They stood facing each other still, each holding a smoking gun. Noah's teeth bared in a cold smile.

'So . . . ' he said.

Then his thick legs buckled and he pitched forward on his face amongst the dead leaves and twigs.

Wade released the breath he had been holding, lifted his left hand and felt the burning wound in his side. But the bullet had passed between his arm and his torso, gouging out a thin layer of flesh, barely enough to make it bleed.

He leaned back against the tree and holstered his Colt, using a sleeve to blot the beads of cold sweat from his forehead.

★ ★ ★

Matthew Wade waited until daylight so that he could track Rocky Calloway by his dust. He was deep in the Sierra here where vegetation was scarce and water was non-existent except to Indians. Geronimo and his renegade Apaches had outwitted him and the army scouts in this country because they knew where the scattered wells were hidden and could live on thorn bushes — while the patrol had to carry all its water and food with them and when it ran out they had no choice but to turn back . . .

Rocky had spotted him coming in and waited on a ridge. Still, playing it safe, he held a cocked rifle when Wade rounded a bend to find the man sitting his mount.

There was a look of disbelief on Calloway's face.

Disbelief mixed with a strange new wariness.

'Expecting Noah?' Wade asked, his throat dry and raspy from the abrading dust.

Rocky put up the rifle and thumbed back his hat.

'What'd you do? Get the drop and shoot him in the back? Or was it a square-off?'

'You want to know what happened, ride back to Alamitos and look at the body.'

Calloway suddenly grinned. 'By Godfrey! You done it, didn't you? You beat that son of a bitch on a square-off!'

Wade reached out and lifted Rocky's canteen from the saddle horn, swigged and rinsed his mouth, spitting between the horses. He corked the canteen and rehung it, all the while looking into Rocky's face.

'He nicked me.' Wade indicated the torn shirt which was barely stained with blood.

'That's all? I gotta shake your hand,

Matt! I tell you, I was nearly comin' back — figurin' I at least owed you a decent burial . . . '

'What stopped you?' Wade made no move to take Rocky's out-thrust right hand.

Calloway frowned, shrugged. 'Figured if you was dead, you was dead and wouldn't care where you was. But then I got to worryin' about how I was gonna find the treasure without your help.'

Wade grinned. 'Sounds more like the Rocky I know.'

He gripped briefly with the man and Calloway's face brightened.

'For a moment there — well, I thought you was about to dissolve the partnership!'

Wade gave him a hard look, then shrugged.

'Decided to renew it. But we'd better move. Get clear of this dust. It's a dead giveaway.'

All the way over the ridges Rocky kept looking at Wade. Sidelong glances followed by a short shake of his head; he was still having trouble believing that his partner had killed Noah . . .

They were wrung out, bodies dry like crushed sponges, by the time sundown came. There had been dust behind them, but it was a long way back and Diego could only have a general direction to follow now without Noah to guide them. By early morning they would be out of the ridges and on to the Llano Blanco, the White Flats. Alkali and still a shortage of water. Not much to look forward to.

They didn't eat because digestion used up body juices. They took small sips of water, the levels dropping in their canteens gradually. They tried not to smoke because that would dry their mouths and worsen their thirst, but the tobacco craving was too much and they each rolled a cigarette and lit up, telling themselves it would help ease the hunger-pangs. Any excuse, as long as they fed the body's craving for nicotine.

' 'Bout time you told me something

about this treasure,' Wade said, his voice hoarse and deeper than usual.

Calloway waved the suggestion away. 'Too damn dry to talk.'

'I need to know, Rocky. Take a drink out of my canteen. We might not have another chance to talk. Diego will be really pushing his men now, you can bet on that.'

Calloway nodded, still not keen, but he did take a drink out of Wade's canteen before he started.

'Dunno all the details, but I've put together the general way of things from what Diego's mentioned from time to time.'

It began with one of his ancestors, a conquistador, with Cortez . . .

His name was José Davila, a true soldier of fortune who had come to Mexico with only one thing in mind: to amass as much gold as possible. He was willing to leave the conversion of the Indians to Christianity to the others; he wanted his reward in this life, not the hereafter.

Just how ruthless he was in gathering his fortune was glossed over by Diego Corzo, according to Calloway, and, in any case, it had little bearing on the rest of the story except that José made more than his share of enemies. But he was a courageous man and fought them all: other conquistadores who coveted his gold, as well as the avenging Aztecs. His hands literally dripped blood but as long as it dripped on piles of gold, José didn't care . . .

There were blank spaces after José began to build his empire and sent to Spain for his long-time *amigo*, Consuela, but it seemed he used a lot of his treasure and, later, after his death, two of his sons fought over the remaining gold. They divided it and each went his own way and the feud continued through various branches of the family until in the early 1800s one part of the scattered family moved back from California — broke, and looking for money from their kinfolk.

They immediately saw the answer to

their financial problems in what remained of the treasure, now under the care of one Don Rafael Corzo. Don Rafé, as he was popularly known, had no intention of sharing what remained of the vast treasure. For sure not with these folk, claiming to be kin, whom he neither knew nor cared for. Violence flared and men — and women — died on both sides.

Then two surviving brothers. José and Angelo, came to their senses. The treasure had passed from hand to hand, juggled back and forth with the fortunes of the feud and now it had been broken up and there was a new danger. Men asserting they were descendants of the original owners, the Aztecs, wanted to reclaim the gold and set about killing the Corzo family one by one, children as well as adults.

José and Angelo hired an assassin to rid them of this menace and the Indians were killed. The brothers were good Catholics and both were sickened by the blood that had been spilled because of this Aztec gold. They decided to put it out of reach of the present family, buried it somewhere near an unnamed lake in the Sierra Madre, drew a map and tore it in two, one half going to each section of the family.

It could be recovered if required, but the Corzo beef and horse empire prospered and the gold was left where it was hidden, for use only in dire emergency. In time, Don Diego took over his family's *rancho*, while Angelo's descendants scattered to the four winds after losing their holdings because of poor investments and gambling. Impoverished, they fled to the United States on money obtained from Don Diego, who bought back their land so as to incorporate it in his holdings, bringing them back almost to the original size claimed by José Davila.

The treasure was not mentioned, which made Don Diego suspicious, but he considered that his generosity also gave him sole rights to that same family treasure. Then, upon investigation he learned that one of the family members had once put up his half of the treasure map to pay a gambling debt, which explained why they had not tried to recover the gold when they were so short of money. After expending his rage, Don Diego become obsessed with the notion of relocating that treasure map and bringing the Aztec gold back into the Corzo family. Its rightful place, in his eyes . . .

'Mighty strong on family ties and honour, is the Don,' Calloway concluded.

'What'd he aim to do with the gold? He can't be short of *dinero*.'

'Hell, no, but that ain't what matters. He looks at it this way: José Davila won that gold as a conquistador. He *stole* it is what he done, pure and simple, but Diego's pride don't let him see it that way. To him, it was the foundation of the Corzo family and their standing amongst the *hidalgos*. He recovers that treasure, and his standing goes through the roof

. . . leastways, that's how he sees it.'

Wade nodded slowly. 'How do you see it, Rock?'

Calloway spread his hands. 'Hell, it don't belong to anybody far as I figure it. It was stole, it was buried, and now it's finders keepers.'

Wade smiled slowly; he'd figured that would be the way Rocky looked at it.

11

Llano Hell

Don Diego's posse was delayed while they buried Noah.

The tough *ranchero* hid his grief as well as he could but there were tears in his eyes and a catch in his voice as he read from a leather-bound bible — which he carried always in his saddle-bags — over the grave. The hired guns, the *pistoleros*, had dug that grave, under protest, on Don Diego's orders, cringing from his rage at their objections.

It was not their job to dig graves, they told him.

After a stream of vituperative Spanish, his face congested with hot blood, the Don had merely pointed to the chosen ground and said, quite softly, 'Dig!'

Pale and reluctant, the men had dug the grave to Don Diego's satisfaction and Noah's body had been wrapped in canvas, buried deep so that prowling mountain lions or coyotes could not reach it, and then rocks were piled upon the mound, a cross made and carved with Noah's name.

Don Diego had stayed behind while the others tidied themselves up — no water was allowed for washing, not in this country and with the type of land that lay ahead — and the *ranchero* swore a solemn oath.

'You will be avenged, Noah. You — will — be avenged!'

Then they had continued into the Sierra, pausing frequently to scan for dust clouds. There was little to go on by now and Steve Kendrick grew impatient, but Don Diego turned to the girl.

'Merida, my dear, you claimed once to have been raised near this country. You have seen the general direction Noah was leading us — what do you think now?'

She was uneasy, looked around in deliberate delay.

'It is many years since I was here, Don Diego . . . ' she gestured. 'The llano lies that way . . . '

'*Sí*, that I know. But this *cienaga*, this swamp — ?'

'I think, south of the llano, far beyond the Alamitos.'

He seemed pleased and gave her a smile and slight inclination of his head. 'Gracias, querida. If you had answered any other way, I might have had your tongue cut out.'

She paled and shivered as Diego turned and urged his men on. Kendrick nudged his horse closer to hers.

'You feel afraid, you can share my blanket tonight. I'll take care of you, *señorita*.' He chuckled.

She turned and spat in his face. 'Take care of that *puerco*! Pig!'

Kendrick lifted a hand to slap at her but froze the blow when he became aware of Don Diego's dark eyes upon him.

'Ride up here with me, Señor Kendrick. I am in need of your opinion as to which trail we should take beyond these poplars . . . '

Kendrick swallowed and spurred his horse forward, his heart pounding.

★ ★ ★

The llano was a gateway to hell — or maybe a piece of that blistering locale itself, misplaced by the devil.

Wade and Calloway hadn't been travelling for long, after starting out in the early grey of daybreak, before their lips were parched and their tongues were sticking to the roofs of their mouths. Alkali coated them, already working into the creases in their flesh and under eyelids, up nostrils, into the corners of their mouths and, of course, beneath clothes.

Calloway did a lot of cussing but Wade kept his mouth closed and didn't waste energy or allow the heat to dry out already parched membranes. Their water tinkled teasingly in the canteens but both men put off touching it. The heat in the sun would soon put it past the palatable stage anyway and they paused long enough to thrust the canteens deep within their bedrolls, protecting the metal from the sun's direct rays. It was an old cavalry trick and while the water was never really cool, at least it didn't scald a man's throat or cause him to wait impatiently until it had cooled sufficiently before taking a drink.

'We gonna make it?' rasped Calloway. 'Or shrivel up like a couple of mummies?'

Matthew Wade didn't answer, merely lifted his arm and pointed ahead into the shimmering haze.

They had a long way to go. A *looooong* way . . .

Calloway had drawn as much of Diego's map as he could remember but Wade was unable to match it up to the part Calloway had located — he deliberately didn't explain just how he had accomplished that particular feat.

Back at last night's camp, Wade had carefully studied the crude drawings and Calloway's portion of the map.

'You sure this is genuine?' he asked.

Calloway had looked directly at him, tried to spit, but his mouth was too dry.

'I wasted a lot of dollars and a lot of bullets if it ain't.'

'Doesn't answer the question.'

Rocky pursed his lips. 'I reckon it's the genuine article. I didn't come by it easy, Matt. It took a long time to trace and I had to . . . get mighty rough. The last man swore it was the real thing . . . just before he died.'

Wade frowned: Rocky had always been a tough *hombre* but he hadn't been cruel or sadistic when they had ridden as pards on the owlhoot trail.

'Mebbe you were a little too rough,' he suggested.

'The hell does that mean?'

'Mebbe the man you were . . . questioning told you just what you wanted to hear so as to save himself a deal more pain.'

Calloway snorted. 'I ain't that big a fool! I soon figured out how much he could take and I never took his first answer as gospel . . . gave him two or three tries. If anythin' — any little thing — was different, he knew what to expect. No, he convinced me that map's the one.'

'Or he believed it was.'

'Judas priest, Matt! The hell're tryin' to do? Look, I was there. I heard him, saw him. He didn't know he was goin' to die, thought he was all set to be turned loose . . . He told the truth.'

Wade's gaze was cold. 'You've gone downhill, Rock.'

Calloway grinned tightly. 'Downhill's easier, ain't you learned that yet?'

'Depends where you're heading — OK. Let's take it as read that this is what we want. It still doesn't show where the treasure's buried. Part of it's missing. It's either on Don Diego's half or it's been torn off.'

199

Calloway was silent for a time.

'Yeah, I been thinkin' that myself. But it was all that could be recovered. I figured if we studied the map, got the general location, then looked for a lake . . . could be in a nearby cave or somethin'. Accordin' to Diego, it'd fill a room in a house, so I can't see 'em buryin' that amount. They'd have to dig too big a hole and in this sort of country . . . '

'Or they could've tossed it *into* the lake.'

Calloway stiffened. 'Christ, I never thought of that!' He shook his head vigorously. 'No. No! They wouldn't do that. They couldn't depend on it bein' safe that way. I mean, lakes dry up in this piece of hell . . . '

'Or deteriorate into swamps!' Wade said suddenly, flicking a finger at the *cienaga* marked on the map. 'South of here there's a *pantano*, a marsh, called Las Colonias. You recall the name of the lake mentioned by Diego's ancestors?'

'They never did name it — that would've been too easy to trace . . . but there was mention of houses, which made me think it wasn't far from a town or village . . .'

'Which could explain the 'Colonias' . . . a bunch of houses . . . I think we ought to head south and check out this marsh, Rocky.'

'You find the way there?'

'I reckon so.'

Calloway grinned through the alkali mask. 'We're on our way to bein' rich, *amigo.* We're on our way!'

But Wade knew they would need plenty of luck to find the treasure with the information they had. *Lots* of luck.

★ ★ ★

They thought of it as the ride through hell, and it seemed endless.

South was no better than the direction they had been heading. In fact the *llano* began to give way to small ridges that reminded them of giant lizards lying out in the baking sun, the tops serrated, a little sand or alkali streaming from them in the furnace wind.

The horses were feeling it and they were given water that the men could not really afford. But the thought of being left afoot in this country made the sacrifice easier.

They had given up speaking to each other altogether, communicating by signs. Calloway was content to follow Wade, knowing he was the pathfinder, had uncanny knowledge of all kinds of wilderness, had won medals in the army for leading patrols through corners of hell and on to eventual salvation. Not that he would ever tell you that; Wade was a man who played everything close to his chest.

And that thought started a little nagging uncertainty deep in Rocky Calloway's mind.

If Wade wanted to, he could lead them into all kinds of trouble and then abandon Calloway, finding his own way out but leaving Calloway to perish ... then Wade could go on and locate the treasure for himself.

But even as the thought formed, Calloway knew it would never happen. It simply wasn't the way Wade operated. He was here now only because it was expedient; he couldn't go back to the States while Roy Engels held that murder charge against him. If they found the treasure, then he would have cash to make a new life for himself south of the border or to travel to California or even South America.

No, there was never any doubt that Wade would share any treasure found; that was how the man was built, he knew no other way.

It had cramped Calloway's style time after time when they had been partners. But this time, he would tag along until he didn't need Wade any more and then he would decide about the treasure. If there was as much as Diego claimed, OK — there would be plenty for them both. But if there wasn't — well, he would have to give the matter some thought.

For this was Calloway's big chance, his only shot at living the easy life. Nothing would make him pass it up when the chips were down. Nothing . . .

* * *

They only just made it out of the *llano*.

Two days in that blistering purgatory and they were like dead men riding. The horses were crossing their legs with each faltering step and the men walked alongside them — *staggered* alongside, gripping the reins tightly, breathing harshly, half-blinded by glare and grit, sucking uselessly on smooth pebbles. There was no saliva left to moisten their mouths.

There was something shimmering way ahead through the haze and at first Wade thought they were houses.

'Town!' he croaked — or tried to but it came out only as a guttural gasp.

In the end he pointed and Calloway

lifted his head tiredly, grunted back and swung in that direction.

But it wasn't a town. It was a collection of giant boulders, the spaces between them almost like streets and laneways, running downhill into a sheet of water reeds where cat's tails waved.

They couldn't believe their eyes as they staggered and stumbled towards the silver sheen. Then the horses increased their pace and drew ahead, leaving the men to stand and stare. It was water all right: the horses smelled it.

Trying to laugh — it was agony for their strictured throats — they linked arms and swayed and zigzagged after the horses, shuffling and staggering, their ungainly pace increasing as they drew closer.

They had found the marsh . . .

★   ★   ★

They were too tired to do much frolicking but once they had slaked their thirst — knowing better than to gulp down a bellyful of water, clear though it was in the deeper pools — they simply flopped back, clothes and all, and let their desiccated bodies soak up the moisture.

Their sixguns were drowned but they didn't care: likely didn't even think about it, the abundance of water filling their minds.

Until, maybe twenty minutes, a half-hour later, when Calloway stopped plunging his scaled face into the pool and burped loudly, shaking his head in an effort to clear water from his eyes.

He rose on one arm and pointed.

'Look!'

Wade, floating face down in the small, deep pool which was becoming stirred up and discoloured now by their antics, lifted his head and squinted against the harsh sun.

There was movement amongst the boulders. Animals and men. At least a dozen men, some riding, some on foot.

All heading in their direction.

Their sixguns had been subjected to too much immersion to be reliable and their rifles were still in their saddle scabbards.

The horses were a hundred feet away, splashing in their own games in an effort to cool off and make the most of the water.

Matthew Wade and Rocky were caught flat-footed.

12

Tesoro!

Some of the men were mounted on burros, some walked. One tall man in front wore an ankle-length brown habit, a dirty white cord gathering the garment around his ample waist, a wooden-and-silver crucifix hanging around his neck on a long brass or gold chain that flashed in the sun.

His hair was grey-white, long and unkempt, his face leathery, the colour of a rifle-butt. He was old but the dark skin was barely lined and the candid blue eyes were startling against his face as he smiled at Wade and Caloway.

'*Buenos dias, señors* . . . I am Padre Manuelo, of the *Misión Abandonada.*' He gestured vaguely to the west and the white men instinctively looked that way, squinting, Wade lifting an arm to shade his eyes.

Now that the grit and alkali had been washed from his eyes and they had been soothed by the marsh water, he saw for the first time the white bell-tower showing above the ridge.

'We didn't notice before, *Padre*,' he said, his voice still hoarse. 'You have a town there?'

'A village only. Some of the faithful.'

'Faithful or abandoned?' asked Wade thinking of the mission's name and Padre Manuelo smiled.

'Once abandoned, perhaps, now faithful, fine Christians. You are welcome to our village. Come, you can dry your clothes and eat good Christian food.'

Calloway glanced at Wade, suspicious, but Wade figured they had little to lose. None of these strangers appeared to be armed, anyway . . .

★   ★   ★

The mission surprised Wade. The paint on the church was fresh and blinding white. The scattered houses were in good repair and corn-patches and other vegetable-gardens seemed well tended and thriving even in this desert.

'We bring water from the marsh with our burros,' the *padre* explained as a couple of matronly women brought them wooden platters of food at a long plank-table. 'We also make our own furniture and I apologize if you find it uncomfortable. But a little discomfort in our daily lives is part of our penance for being sinners.'

Wade frowned as he bit into a *tortilla*. 'Not you, surely, *padre*?'

'We are all sinners, my son. If we are born into this world, we carry a burden of sin and must atone for it during our lifetime. That is the way of our faith.'

The white men were given rough-woven cotton robes to wear while the women washed and dried their clothes. Both men felt uneasy when their gun rigs were taken away with the clothes and later they found them drying in the sun.

The weapons had been disassembled and the individual parts spread out on a blanket, also the cartridges. They glittered in the hot sunlight.

Wade wondered who amongst the *padre*'s flock knew how to dismantle Colt pistols so expertly . . .

After they had eaten, Padre Manuelo took them on a tour of the church, showing them the fine hand-carved timbers of the altar with its golden chalices and crosses, the sacristy lamp, incense burners and a gold-edged lectern.

'A lot of gold here, Father,' commented Calloway tightly and Manuelo smiled.

'If only that were true, *señor*. If only we could show our Lord how much we revered Him by decorating our church and its poor offerings with gold! Alas, *señor*, it is only brass. The special paste made from the desert alkali by our artisans imparts that rich, deep polish.

Many people have mistaken it for gold. You will see our forge and small brass-foundry later.'

Calloway frowned, and picked up a small etched cross set on a red mahogany base. He rubbed the metal, turned it this way and that to catch the light. The *padre* watched, smiling easily.

'It is very misleading, eh, *señor*?'

'Yeah. It would've fooled me if you hadn't told me that it was brass. I'd like to see your foundry.'

'Of course. It operates only occasionally, but you will see the sand-moulds and the beeswax we use for all the shapes you see now on our altar.' He swept his arm around abruptly, the dangling sleeve flapping. 'Come, I will show you my library. I pride myself on following the old-time monks and illuminating the pages of our Bible which I am making from parchment made here by us. I am copying the full text by hand, a laborious but gratifying task.'

Now that was *real* devotion, thought

Wade, following the *padre*; writing out the hundreds of thousands of words in the Bible by hand . . . this was one devout Christian.

Or one highly-repentant sinner desperately seeking atonement . . .

★ ★ ★

The leisurely tour of the village went on into the afternoon and when they returned to the main building their clothes were waiting for them, washed and pressed, and their weapons had been assembled and oiled.

'You have a gunsmith amongst your flock, *Padre*?' Wade asked checking his Colt, as did Calloway with his gun.

Manuelo smiled, spreading his hands.

'We have converts from all walks of life. Talents from their previous lives can be of use here but now they are used for the Lord's work.' He gestured to their guns. 'You obviously feel you need protection, so we have restored your weapons to working order.'

'You're very trusting, Father,' Calloway said, sounding a little bored.

'Our Lord was a trusting man, señor.'

'Yeah and look where it got him . . . '

Wade frowned and shook his head at Calloway and the man cut off whatever else he was about to say.

The *padre*'s smile had vanished, but returned in a few moments.

'You are welcome to spend the night here, *amigos*.'

'Only one night?' Calloway asked slyly.

'That is not sufficient? Then stay by all means — as long as you wish.' Manuelo moved his clear blue eyes from one man's face to the other. 'There is something I can help you with, perhaps?'

'You've been a good help already, *Padre*,' Wade told him. 'You haven't even asked why we are here.'

'You will tell me if you wish me to know. But you needed help after crossing the *llano*. Why you crossed it if of no matter.'

Calloway spoke out of the corner of his mouth as the *padre* led the way outside to the small village plaza.

'This *hombre*'s too good to be true.'

'Don't push your luck, Rocky. He might know something of the treasure, but we'll have to be careful how we question him . . . '

'Yeah, well, all this — . Judas priest!'

They were outside now, stepping into the small plaza where it seemed that several of the villagers had gathered.

Then they parted and out of the shadows of the huts rode a band of horsemen, led by a smiling Don Diego Corzo, flanked on one side by Steve Kendrick, and on the other by Merida.

The *pistoleros* behind him held cocked rifles.

'So, at last we have caught up with you, Mateo, Roca!' Diego was pleased with himeelf and indicated the silent and sober girl. 'Thanks to Merida! She knew this country better than she had led us to believe and found a short cut that brought us here. Just at the right time, it seems.'

'I am sorry, Mateo!' burst out the girl, looking anguished. 'He make me!'

Wade nodded, not taking his eyes off Diego. 'That's all right, Merida. Now what, Diego? We're all here. Are we all going to look for the treasure?'

'*Tesoro*!' exclaimed the *padre*,' looking from Wade and Calloway to the newcomers. 'You seek treasure? *Here*?'

'Somewhere near here, *Padre*,' answered Diego quietly. 'My ancestors hid it long ago. Now I have come to reclaim it.'

Manuelo was silent a moment and then smiled faintly as he nodded. 'Ah, I see. You know where to find your *tesoro*, then?'

'Not yet.' Diego looked directly at Calloway. 'My friend Roca knows, I think. He will show me.'

Calloway shook his head. 'Out of luck, Diego. There's a piece of the map missin'. We'll have to guess.'

'As long as it is a good guess, Roca.'

There was a touch of menace in the Don's quiet rejoinder. He straightened in the saddle, moving a little stiffly. '*Padre*, you can offer me and my friends your hospitality for the night?'

Manuelo spread his arms. 'Our village is yours. We can give you food and shelter — and prayers for those who wish them.'

'*I* will accept that offer, *Padre*. I wish to give thanks for our deliverance from the Sierra. As to the others . . . they must decide for themselves.'

'You'll like the altar, Diego,' Calloway said and though the rancher waited with arched eyebrows for him to continue. Rocky said no more.

'I will post my men to stand guard around your village, *Padre*,' Diego said casually. 'We glimpsed *bandidos* to the north on our way in.'

'Bandits do not trouble us, *señor*. We are harmless, live our simple lives and trouble no one.'

'But you do not usually have rich visitors,' Diego said with a slight bow, indicating himself. 'They may well be tempted. My men will stand guard. But I think Mateo and Roca should give me their weapons to look after.'

The *padre* seemed puzzled by the request but he frowned when the rifles of the *pistoleros* swung to cover the two Texans.

'This I do no understand, *señor* . . . '

'No need to, *Padre* — I am in charge while we are here. You have no objection?'

No humble mission *padre* would dare challenge the authority of a self-styled *hidalgo*, so Manuelo merely bowed his head. Then Diego snapped his fingers impatiently and Rocky and Wade reluctantly unbuckled their gun belts.

Steve Kendrick kneed his mount forward, grinned as he reached down and took the weapons.

'Nice to see you again, Matt.'

'Where's Engels?'

'In Laredo. He couldn't officially come after you.'

'So he sent you to do the dirty work.'

'Work? More like a pleasure, *amigo*, pure pleasure!'

Merida's white teeth tugged at her bottom lip as she watched Wade anxiously . . .

★　★　★

After supper the bell rang for the angelus and Don Diego dutifully rose from the long plank-table and went into the church. The armed guard who had been standing by during supper tensed and clutched his rifle more tightly, watching Wade and Calloway closely.

Now that Diego was occupied with his devotions, Merida, who had been sitting at his side during the meal, changed places and wriggled in on the plank-seat between Wade and Kendrick. Her small hand sought Wade's.

'I did not wish to bring trouble upon you, Mateo.'

'I know, Merida. And I know how

persuasive Diego can be. Don't worry about it.'

She squeezed his hand, looking into his face. His expression didn't change but there was a slight flare of hope in his eyes.

'Just don't get your hopes up, Matt,' Kendrick said, leaning forward. 'You ain't walkin' away from this. That's why I'm here. If I can cut myself in for a share of the treasure, fine, but my prime purpose is to take care of you.'

Wade held his stare but said nothing. The girl looked perturbed. Calloway didn't appear to be listening but Wade knew he had heard every word and intonation of the brief conversation.

Then they were all startled by the reappearance of Don Diego, with Padre Manuelo gripped tightly by one arm. He pushed the priest down the short flight of steps into the plaza, now lit by flickering resinous pine-branches fixed at intervals on the walls of the mission.

The villagers stirred, surged forward, but stopped when the *pistoleros* stepped forward, menacing them with their guns.

Diego looked at Wade and Calloway. 'The *padre* has just assured me that the altar's vessels are made of brass and not gold, as I believed.'

'It is the truth, Don Diego!' Manuelo said a little tightly; no doubt the rancher's grip was painful. 'I will gladly show you our small foundry and our stocks of zinc and copper, together with the moulds used . . .'

For a moment Diego looked uncertain, then his law tightened. 'You will do that, *padre*. And you will do it now!'

He barked an order to two of his men and they broke away, flanking the priest. The villagers stirred restlessly and Manuelo called to one man to join him while he showed Don Diego the small foundry.

'Sounds mighty interestin',' opined Kendrick. 'I reckon you two have had enough to eat.' He stood abruptly, his gun sliding out of leather, the hammer cocking. 'Relax, Matt! I won't kill you yet. But you and Calloway are gonna be locked up for the night. Merida, you get outta the way and stay here. I'll take care of this chore.'

The girl sat there silently as Kendrick marched Wade and Calloway out of the crowded plaza to the adobe corn store which had only one small door although there were several tiny ventilation holes high up in the walls. He pushed them inside and closed the heavy door, dropping the bar across.

'You won't go hungry anyway,' he chuckled. 'Or you can amuse yourselves trying to catch some of the rats!'

Laughing, he moved away, leaving Wade and Calloway in almost total darkness. Only a very faint light drifted in through the ventilation holes, which were only large enough for a man to push his closed fist through.

'Wouldn't want to be that *padre*,' Calloway allowed, finding a sack of corn-cobs to sit on.

'Why's that?'

'Diego's no fool. He knows gold

when he sees it.'

'That *is* gold then? All that stuff in the church?'

'Hell, did you ever doubt it?'

'Guess I believed the *padre* . . . although I reckon I had my suspicions.'

''Course it's real gold! He showed us the moulds, right? Broken open and left lyin' around to gather dust, just for such a time as this when someone needed convincin' it's only brass.'

'Well, the moulds were all the right shape and size . . . '

Calloway snorted. 'Yeah. But I looked at some of them chalices pretty damn close. They still show the original hammer marks from where they were beaten out.'

Wade was silent for a few moments. 'By the Aztec goldsmiths, you mean?'

'Yeah. They ain't been moulded. They were handbeaten! That crafty old sonuver of a *padre* must've found the treasure sometime and used it in the church. The crosses have been made from melted-down metal, but the other vessels have had some of the Aztec turquoise and gems removed and used to decorate other stuff. I'd stake my life on it.'

'That's exactly what you're doing, Rock. If Manuelo convinces Diego those vessels are only made of brass, he's gonna string us up by the thumbs and torture us till we tell him where we think the treasure is — or die.'

'Son of a bitch! Why'd that Mex slut have to lead him in here!'

'Don't blame her — you know how Diego can be better than I do. What we've got to do is find a way out — and get our hands on our guns.'

Calloway snorted again. 'You put so much faith in the *padre*, why don't you ask him to say a prayer for us? It's got as much chance of workin' as anythin' else!'

Wade didn't answer. Because he figured Calloway was right.

★ ★ ★

Diego wasn't satisfied. The moulds matched the shapes of the altar vessels, all right; there were even moulds for the crosses. But he knew gold when he saw it, touched it. Nothing else had the same feel as gold . . .

He ordered one of his gunmen to fetch something from amongst the altar's vessels, anything, as long as it was metal. The man brought back a wine-chalice and Diego carried it close to a lantern that had been lit and set on a table in the plaza.

The rest of his men had ordered the villagers to return to their homes, telling them to stay there until daylight or they would be shot on sight.

'There!' Diego said suddenly, peering more closely into the interior of the vessel, touching the lower part with a fingertip. 'I can feel it now! Hammer marks! This never came from any mould! It was hammered out by a smith!'

'*Sí*, one or two were made by hand,' explained the *padre* coolly. 'At that time we had an old silversmith in our community but he has since gone to his reward in heaven. It was after his death that we started pouring the molten brass into moulds . . . '

Diego spun and raised his hand as if to strike the old priest and while Manuelo flinched he did not cower. The rancher hesitated, thought better of hitting a man of God, and lowered his fist slowly.

'You lie to me, old man.'

'Those vessels have been blessed, sanctified, for many years. They belong to God now! It matters not whether they are base metal or gold or silver or anything else. They are God's vessels, Don Diego. It would be a great sin for you to steal them, or to cause harm to anyone because of them.'

'Don't you threaten me with hellfire and damnation, you sanctimonious old fool!' raged the Don, flushing, his hands trembling a little. But he was quick to set down the chalice on the plank-table, staring at it, his face taut and pale. 'You are the one who is lying! This is my gold! My ancestor José Davila earned it by right of conquest! It must come back into my family! And it will!'

'I know nothing of that of which you speak, Don Diego.'

Diego's face was ugly as he stood and locked gazes with the padre. 'But I think you do, Padre.'

Manuelo almost smiled. 'What will you do? Torture me? I must warn you now that the villagers won't stand for that. Whatever else you may think I may be, I am a man of God and I do His work in this place . . .'

Muscles worked along Diego's jaw. He badly wanted to assault the priest but his religious beliefs prevented him. There was the fear that any man who maltreated a priest would be eternally damned.

Then he smiled, coldly.

'I will not harm you, Padre. But you have a whole village full of friends who are no more than peons. Perhaps some of them will tell me what I want to know or beg *you* to tell me when they can stand my ... questioning no more.' He laughed briefly. 'We will all sleep on it, eh? Who knows what tomorrow might bring? Perhaps your collaboration, perhaps not. For a while, I suspect — well, *buenos noches, Padre.*'

He snapped orders to one of his men and the priest was led away. Kendrick came across.

'Any luck?'

'We will see ... we will see.'

*　★　★　★*

They stacked the sacks of corn-cobs high against one wall until Wade, standing precariously atop them, could reach one of the ventilation holes. As he had suspected, the mud was softer here, flaky, having been protected from the baking sun by the overhang of the roof. He took off his right spur and began to dig.

The mud came away in dollar-sized flakes. It was still harder than he had expected but they had all night, and there were two of them . . .

13

God's Gold

There were no guards patrolling regularly but an armed *pistolero* did make the rounds from time to time. Wade and Calloway were careful to brush the flaked mud inside the corn store so the guard would not see it on the ground.

It was slow work, hard and hot, and they were soaked in sweat long before they had a hole large enough to get their heads and shoulders through. By then it was very late; they had been forced to take a break, the heat was so bad in the ill-ventilated corn store.

Time had gotten away from them because, in their exhausted state, they had fallen asleep while resting. They worked harder once they were awake again and twice the guard came but he didn't see anything even though he looked up. The part of the wall they worked on was deep in the shadow cast by the roof's overhang.

There was the faintest suggestion of grey in the east when they wriggled through the hole and dropped soundlessly to the ground.

Wade checked one corner of the store while Calloway checked the other. No sign of the guard. They figured that now it was close to getting light the man would not check so frequently. During their exit, they had brought down some clods that had shattered upon striking the ground. There was little they could do about it so they made their way towards the silent church.

'We need our guns!' hissed Calloway, grabbing Wade's arm.

'Talk about it inside!'

They eased into the church proper, into that strange comforting silence of a darkened and deserted House of God. A dim light glowed in an overhead incensory and the always-burning sacristy lamp.

Even such a dim light reflected from the deep yellowish metal of the altar vessels.

Wade froze as Calloway reached under his jacket and brought out an empty sack.

'Where'd you get that?'

'The corn store. Figured it might come in handy.'

Calloway started for the altar but Wade's restraining grip on his arm brought him around swiftly.

'Leave it.'

'You loco? Now's our chance to grab it and get out of here!'

'There's too much to carry.'

'Then we'll take what we can manage. I ain't leavin' all this for Don Diego. I've lost a lot of sweat and smelled a lot of powdersmoke over the years, just waitin' for this moment, Matt. Don't try to stop me now.'

'That's just what I am gonna do. It's not ours, Rocky. Nor Don Diego's, either.'

'Well, it sure ain't Padre Manuelo's!

He might've found it but . . . '

'You said 'finders keepers' not so long ago.'

'Well. We looked for the treasure and now we've found it. So we take it and keep it.' His voice hardened, echoing around the high-vaulted church. 'Leastways, *I* do!'

'Forget it, Rocky. We'll be lucky to get away with our lives, let alone trying to carry out a sackful of gold.'

'Get out of my way, Matt!'

Calloway went to step around Wade, thrusting with his left hand. Wade stepped slightly to one side and then blocked his path again. Calloway didn't hesitate: he swung the empty sack and it took Wade across the face, the dust from within the coarse hessian fibres half-blinding and choking him.

Calloway hit him hard on the back of the neck as Wade doubled over, coughing, and the man spread out on the cold slate floor. Rocky stepped over him and began pushing the altar vessels and crosses into the sack. They clinked but he didn't worry about the noise; cramming as much into the sack as he could was all that interested him now . . .

Wade still hadn't moved by the time he had finished, reluctantly forced to leave some bulky items on the altar.

He glanced down at Wade's dark shape, threw him a casual salute as he made for the side door.

'*Adios, amigo.* You always were too damn honest for my liking.'

He made it out through the door and a few steps beyond into the grey dimness of the new day. Then he heard the sound behind him. Calloway spun, swore softly when he saw Wade lurching against the door-frame, shaking his head groggily.

Without a word, Wade charged and Calloway swung the heavy sack. Matthew Wade warded off the blow with his left arm and the vessels clunked and clanged as the sack fell to the ground. Wade's arms went about Calloway's hips and carried the man over backwards. Rocky kicked and thrashed as Wade buried his head up under the man's chin, still trying to regain his full senses.

He rammed a knee into Calloway's belly and the man faltered, grunting. Wade kicked free and both men stumbled as they got to their feet. Calloway bared his teeth, rushed back in, swinging. Wade caught two blows on his lower arms and a third grazed his jaw. Then he ducked under the next swing, hammered a tattoo on Calloway's midriff. Rocky staggered back, one leg buckling. He wavered drunkenly and fell to one knee, started up almost at once — and ran full-on into a whistling left hook that stretched him out on the ground. He fell across the sack, and some of the vessels crumpled, screeching along the inlaid stones of the path.

He rolled on to his back as Wade closed, kicked upwards, sending the freighter stumbling back.

And suddenly there were running

sounds and shouts and the two men were surrounded by Diego's gunmen. The Don himself came running up, hair awry, a gun in his hand. There was enough light to see his crooked smile and also the marks of battle on the faces of Calloway and Wade.

'So. You are convinced they are gold after all, Roca!' Diego gestured to the sack where several chalices had spilled on to the ground. He rounded on the *padre* who had come up quietly. 'Manuelo, you have been a bad man, I think.'

'Don Diego, I told you. These things belong to God, whatever they are made of!'

'Perhaps. But there should be a lot more of my ancestor's treasure, *Padre*. What have you done with it?'

Manuelo said nothing, and was surprised to see Diego grin.

'I see you have reached your decision. Very well, so have I.' He looked at the head *pistolero*, a moustached youngish man in *vaquero's* clothing. 'Cimarron, burn those three houses. At once! Do not give the *peons* time to remove anything. Just burn them!'

There were cries of alarm from the sleepy villagers who were gathering as Cimarron and another man snatched one of the still flickering resinous pine-boughs from the side of the mission and ran for the houses. Clawing hands tried to stop them but were beaten aside with gun-metal. A woman began to wail. A man called on the *padre* for help . . .

Diego looked quizzically at the priest. 'It is in your power to stop this, Manuelo. You know you only need to tell me what I want to know. If you don't by the time the first three houses are burned to the ground, we will burn three more. After that, the mission and the church. Then you will have no use for altar vessels, brass *or* gold.'

Manuelo released a long sigh as he saw Cimarron preparing to touch his torch to the thatched roof of the nearest house.

'Stop them, Don Diego,' he said lifelessly. 'I will tell you what you wish to know.'

Smiling in triumph, Diego called his orders to Cimarron and his helper and they stood back, still holding the burning torches. He turned to the *padre*.

'And now, Manuelo . . . ?'

The father's shoulders were slumped.

'The *padre* who was here before me found the treasure. In the marsh, before it had shrunk to a series of pools as it is today. He was a fisherman and hooked up some of the golden objects. Some of the villagers dived and retrieved what they could and the father himself tried to recover what remained but it was too deep. He died from his efforts and the villagers were afraid to touch the treasure they had already brought up. They hid it and I was here for several years before they eventually showed it to me . . . '

'What about the unrecovered treasure?' asked Diego impatiently.

Manuelo held up a hand.

'There was beauty in many of the heathen objects and although at first I was tempted to smash them and throw them back into the marsh and let them sink in the quicksand, I decided to sanctify them and put them to God's service . . . '

'Yes, yes, I understand that!' broke in the Don. 'But the unrecovered gold! It is still there? In the marsh?'

'I think it must be.'

'*Think*! You *know*, old man! And you will tell me now!'

'Don Diego, the lake has shrunk. There have been many years of drought. Much of the marsh is quicksand and mud. There is no treasure in any of the pools, I assure you. The water is crystal clear. You can see for yourself. I believe that what gold was left has sunk down into the mud and quicksand and is lost for ever . . . '

Diego's nostrils flared. His dark eyes widened. He stared for a long minute at the *padre* who faced him squarely, even though he must have known he was but a breath or two from Eternity. He fingered his crucifix and his lips moved in a silent prayer as he prepared to meet his Maker.

Wade and Calloway had been virtually forgotten, everyone concentrating on the priest as he spoke. Everyone except Merida, who had come creeping around the far side of the mission, carrying two holstered Colts with the bullet belts wrapped about them.

While everyone waited for Diego to decide what he was going to do with Manuelo, she came up silently behind Wade and Calloway, pressed the gun rigs into their hands. They took them without looking at her, used the crowd for cover as they swiftly buckled on the weapons.

But Steve Kendrick chose that moment to swivel his gaze towards Wade, still intent on his main job of seeing that the man did not live to tell about his gun-running.

'What the hell! Watch out, Don Diego!'

Kendrick snatched at his gun and it was almost clear of leather before Wade's rig was settled firmly enough for him to attempt a draw. He dropped to one knee, sweeping the Colt out of the holster, his left hand striking the hammer spur, trigger-finger depressing simultaneously so that the gun fired when the hammer fell.

Kendrick staggered, spinning half away, twisting back, teeth bared as he brought up his own gun. Wade's second shot took him in the chest and smashed him backwards into the scattering crowd.

Cimarron and his men started shooting, bringing down two villagers in their hurry to pick off Wade. Calloway was fanning his gun hammer and two of Cimarron's men went down kicking. Cimarron himself swung his gun on Wade but Matt shot him through the face, wounded another man beside him, then swung his gun on to Diego.

The Don had grabbed hold of the *padre* and held the man in front of him like a shield, but his gun was pointed at Merida who crouched, afraid to move, mesmerized by the muzzle of the weapon that threatened her.

'I believe I have the advantage, Mateo! Now drop your gun! You, too, Roca!'

Wade hesitated, then let his gun fall at his feet. Diego swung his gun towards Calloway.

'Roca!'

But Calloway shook his head.

'No, Diego, I don't care about the gal nor the *padre*! Not even you!'

His gun blasted and Diego staggered back away from the *padre*. Merida screamed. Wade dived for his sixgun, scooped it up, shoulder-rolled and came up on one knee facing Calloway who was beading him coldly. They fired together.

When the gunsmoke cleared, Calloway was down on his knees, a hand clawed into his chest, a thin trickle of blood at a corner of his mouth. His eyes were wide as he stared at Wade.

'Damn you, Matt! You still have . . . that killer instinct . . . '

He tumbled forward and spread out on his face. The girl ran to Wade as he stood erect and he slipped an arm about her slim waist.

'Oh, Mateo! Mateo!' she gasped but he turned his gaze to where Diego was sitting on the ground, looking at the blood on his hand where it was pressed into his side. The *padre* looked up from examining the wound.

'He will live, *señor*.'

'You sure you want him to, *padre*?' Wade asked and Manuelo regarded him in surprise.

'Of course!'

'He'll take your gold.'

The *padre* sighed. 'Perhaps it may be as well . . . '

'No,' Diego gasped, shaking his head.

'No. I was wrong. The *padre* is right. It belongs to God now.' He smiled thinly. 'I give it to Him. It was mine and now I give it to Padre Manuelo's church in the service of God. It must earn me credit in heaven, eh, *Padre*?'

'Only God can answer that, Don Diego.'

Wade left them to it, reloading his gun as he looked down at Calloway.

'You will go back to Laredo now?' asked Merida, but he shook his head.

'Engels will still have that murder charge on me. I'll square things one day, but not for a long time, I think.'

'Then what will you do?'

He shrugged. 'Rocky was right. I still have the killer instinct. Once it earned me a right good living. Dangerous, but lucrative.'

'You will return to this way?'

It was a straight question, without surprise nor censure.

'Don't see I have a choice, Merida. Guess it was always meant that I make my own way to hell.'

She stared, frowning, then slipped a hand through his arm.

'I think I have seen this hell from time to time, but I am not sure. I will come with you and we will find this place together.'

He looked down into her beautiful young face and smiled faintly.

'Well, maybe we'll find a better place — if we look together.'

Her teeth flashed in the first rays of the new sun and her grip tightened on his arm.

'This I am sure of, Mateo! Very sure!'

THE END

Soon the paddle-steamer would be on its long journey down the Missouri River to St Louis. Now, all Saul Rhymer had to do was to play the last master-stroke of the evening. He looked at the mounting pile of gold and dollar bills and again at the cards in his hand. Then, looking around the table, he produced the deed to the goldmine in Montana. 'Let's play poker!' But little did he know how that journey back to St Louis would change his life so drastically.

THE ARIZONA KID

Andrew McBride

When former hired gun Calvin Taylor took the job of sheriff of Oxford County, New Mexico, it was for one reason only — to catch, or kill, the notorious Arizona Kid, and pick up the fifteen hundred dollars reward the governor had secretly offered. Taylor found himself on the trail of the infamous gang known as the Regulators, hunting down a man who'd once been his friend. The pursuit became, in every sense, a journey of death.

BULLETS IN BUZZARDS CREEK

Bret Rey

The discovery of a dead saloon girl is only the beginning of Sheriff Jeff Gilpin's problems. Fortunately, his old friend 'Doc' Holliday arrives in Buzzards Creek just as Gilpin is faced by an outlaw gang. In a dramatic shoot-out the sheriff kills their leader and Holliday's reputation scares the hell out of the others. But it isn't long before the outlaws return, when they know Holliday is not around, and Gilpin is alone against six men . . .

THE YANKEE HANGMAN

Cole Rickard

Dan Tate was given a virtually impossible task: to save the murderer Jack Williams from the condemned cell. Williams, scum that he was, held a secret that was dear to the Confederate cause. But if saving Williams would test all Dan's ingenuity, then his further mission called for immense courage and daring. His life was truly on the line and if he didn't succeed, Horace Honeywell, the Yankee Hangman would have the last word!